GW01179630

THE BITER BIT

and other tales.

A Collection of 22 Short Stories

Harry Downey

ISBN 928-0-244-06110-4

THE AUTHOR.

Harry Downey had a working career in production planning and industrial management before a he made a lifestyle change in 1980, after which he and his late wife dealt in antiques for many years.

Originally after retirement he regularly wrote reviews of classical music CD's for a major website, but has now returned to an early interest in writing fiction.

Born in Lancashire and remarried, he now lives in West Dorset.

He can be contacted at *harry.downey372@gmail.com*

Beaminster. December 2017

Books by Harry Downey

***Tie a yellow ribbon**. A crime novel involving two clever scams, theft from a London gang boss and the inevitable hunt for revenge and retribution that follows.*

***Time for a short?** A collection of 22 short stories previously published separately in various magazines.*

***The biter bit and other stories.** A second volume with 21 short stories previously published separately in various magazines.*

***'If at first.....'** A novella. George is a pathetic figure who wants to dispose of his wife and replace her with a younger model. With an increasingly fuddled mind, and being the loser he is, nothing goes quite as planned, even though he has the support of Winston Churchill in person.*

ABOUT THIS BOOK.

This is a new edition of a book published in 2015 under the same title. That edition has been withdrawn and replaced by this one, with a handful of minor revisions and with the addition of an extra story – number 15 in the index.

The basis of the choice of tales included remains the same. Each and every one has been published in one of the UK's small-press literary print or online magazines over recent years. So the selection of stories to include was not strictly mine, but only if an editor considered it worth publishing in his/her magazine will it appear in these pages. This is most definitely not an indiscriminate selection of a self indulgent author.

One thing remains unchanged. Most of these small publications are run by enthusiasts in their own time and often on a shoe-string budget and many fall by the wayside. To the survivors and to those who haven't made it, I want to offer my thanks.

H.D. **December 2017**

CONTENTS.

THE BITER BIT.

(Published in *Fiction on the Web*.
January 2014).

ONE.

As Charlie was just about to offer up his customary incantation about 'the first of the evening' Freddie came up to him and offered to buy him a pint. Freddie was known as a man with 'short arms and deep pockets' – so Charlie realised something unusual was in the offing.

Freddie was a whippet of a man compared to Charlie's massive six feet three with matching bulk, so his whispered *'I'd like a word on the Q.T. please Charlie,'* wasn't easy to hear even in a half-empty bar. Charlie would have preferred to remain where he was, but seeing the pleading look that Freddie gave him he pointed to an empty table and they went across and sat down. Even though there was no risk of being overheard, he still looked around carefully before speaking to match Freddie's obvious concern.

'What's the matter, Freddie? You look like a man with problems. Tell your Uncle Charlie all about it.' Freddie didn't seem to hear – just sat there looking anxious with such an 'I'm feeling sorry for myself' look that Charlie felt tempted to shake him out of it.

After what seemed like minutes of this Freddie pulled a postcard from his inside pocket and passed it over for Charlie to read.

It was a standard, touristy-type card with views of London – coloured pictures of Tower Bridge, Big Ben, Buckingham Palace – that sort of thing. The postmark was blurred but he thought it was E15 – a district he remembered slightly from years before. Not up to much then, but possibly peopled by millionaires these days the way property prices had gone.

'Never knew your surname before, Freddie. Are you named after the zoo or is it the other way round?'

That attempt at cheering him up fell flat too so Charlie read the card in silence. The message was brief and handwritten – in a scrawl that wasn't easy to read.

'Freddie, old boy.

Haven't heard from you for a while. I thought we were going to keep in touch. Not thought of moving on again without letting me have an address, have you? I know you wouldn't do that to an old friend. I still have the note you and Elsie left with me. Money's a bit tight down here so another little advance by return would be welcome.'

There was no signature.

He passed the card back.

'Come on Freddie, my seat is getting cold and you know I like to sit there where I can philosophise and watch the world go by. Well, sit at the bar anyway. The card's nothing to get worked up about. Explain everything or I'm off. Chop, chop.'

'Point taken Charlie. Just bear with me while I get you that pint then all will be made clear.'

The first time you heard it, Freddie's voice came as a surprise. In this small Derbyshire town where the local accent was strong and ugly, Freddie's carefully modulated tones and enunciation that Charlie had heard referred to in the bar as '*very Daily Telegraph*' stood out.

Charlie's own accent had changed to come closer to that of his companion. This modification was almost instinctive by now, and owed much to his time as a young man at Drama School and afterwards in repertory companies, progressing to being a minor name in the West End, TV and in occasional films. Over the years he had found that he easily took on an accent and speech pattern that was right for the company he was with at the time.

His background had also left him with a range of impressions – not earth shattering, Charlie knew his limitations – but decent enough to entertain at the occasional fund-raising show for local charities. Charlie was especially proud of three of his voices – people seemed to like his Basil Fawlty – and that gift for impressionists everywhere, Michael Caine.

His *'piece of resistance'* as he called it was Sean Connery. It was so good that Charlie had once been asked to dub the Scotsman's voice in a comedy television advert, but he turned it down, even though Connery himself had given his permission. The fee was very generous and afterwards Charlie often regretted his refusal. Particularly when the ad was made and screened. It made quite a stir in the press when the news slipped out – or was more probably deliberately leaked to get a little bit more publicity – that it wasn't the Scot himself but one of the country's top impressionists who was being paid a small fortune for the voiceover. Charlie's professionally objective view was that he could have done it himself just as well.

***

Freddie came back from the bar with a pint of local bitter and his own preferred drink – a glass of red wine. The two men were not in danger of being overheard but still Freddie looked around closely before he began to speak.

‘It’s like this.’ He sipped his wine as a connoisseur would, but clearly from his grimace the house red was not a wine-buff’s vintage of choice.

‘The man who sent me the card is blackmailing me. He’s saying that a fresh payment is due and warning me not to try to move on as he will trace me. Really he says a lot in a single card if you know how to read it.’

Charlie chose not to interrupt and Freddie carried on. Again he glanced around at his neighbours – none of whom could have heard him but he kept his voice low when he next spoke.

‘I have a record – a police record. I did time about five years ago for embezzling some money from an employer. I have no complaints about it – I did wrong, was caught, and punished for it. You’ll have to take my word for it that since I came out I have been clean.’

‘Point taken Freddie. I’ve always found you OK and if you say you’re straight now, of course I’ll take your word for it. I assume we’re speaking in confidence about your past? ‘

‘Indeed we are. Apart from me, you are now the only person in Heanor who knows what I have just told you. I may be here for a while yet so I want to keep it quiet.’

‘That’s alright, Freddie. It’ll go no further – but why are you telling me?’

Charlie was getting interested. Life was routine these days and he needed some variety. Here he was – no regular job, just the odd bits and pieces his agent found him. They helped to top up his savings and as he had never been an extravagant person he managed to get by – with a few years to go until pension date he couldn’t splash out much.

The trouble was that if he got the occasional odd part, or a couple of lines in a sit-com or a walk-on bit in the pub scene in a soap, when finally they were seen on the box, somehow his jobs seemed to be screened closely together. So when the regulars in *The Nag's Head* saw him on the TV they assumed he had masses of work. If only. Those two tiny jobs could have been after months 'resting' (the old euphemism easily came back to him).

'Let me tell you some more and then we'll talk about where you might fit in if you agree to help me out Charlie.'

'You can probably appreciate, that with a police record, job openings are restricted. You don't know my background but my family is what you might call 'upper crust' and has pots of money. They gave me an expensive education, and it was always assumed by the family that I'd just potter along until the time came to inherit – I'm an only child. This family assumption didn't include asking my opinion on the future, so when I left Eton and went on to Cambridge, after a year and a bit I chucked it all and just drifted for a while. I was determined to make my own way in the world without the family money, so I took on the job in that office that eventually put me into gaol.'

'When I came out things were pretty iffy until finally I got a job of sorts with a fellow called Solomons – Jonty Solomons. He's a car dealer in East London. He has a pitch where he sells second hand vehicles, and does all his repairs and stuff in one of those places you see in those crime programmes on the telly – under those massive railway arches. You know the sort of place.'

Indeed he did. Oh, the number of those garages under the arches that Charlie had gone into dressed in blue in his time. The memories came flooding back. He tried to push them away to concentrate on the man in front of him.

As Freddie told his tale and Charlie listened, taking the occasional sip from his pint, he studied this interesting character who had appeared from nowhere some months earlier. He first met him here in the pub when he saw him sitting alone in a corner. He was dressed then – as now – in a dark blue suit, the sort the locals would sometimes refer to as an 'interview suit', except that it was of a better cut and quality than your average *'Nag's Head'* punter would ever wear or could even probably afford. In his early thirties, about five feet six, slightly built, pale rather than sallow skinned with regular features that some might regard as feminine. In a *'short back and sides'* pub his longish fair hair parted on the right with carefully combed wings at each ear was certainly different. An open neck blue shirt, no tie but a matching blue handkerchief draping casually from his breast pocket added to the effect.

The reaction of many of the regulars was obvious and their views were strengthened the moment he opened his mouth. *'Posh queer probably looking for a bit of rough'*. Almost inevitably with an opinion like that of the newcomer, he was avoided at first in the pub, but when Charlie started to have the occasional chat with Freddie and others too found he was worth talking to, he became generally accepted as one of the regulars. This assimilation was helped when one evening he was dragooned into the pub *'Quiz Nite'* team and helped it to a decisive win over the team from *'The Barley Mow'*. Freddie clearly knew about matters that were way beyond the knowledge of his team-mates and his status in the pub shot up as a result.

Freddie did drop one clanger though. In a way that clearly was normal to him he referred to the landlord just by his surname. *'Another one in there, please, Garthrop, there's a good chap'* – and you could have heard the proverbial pin as it hit the floor. There was a heated exchange that finally was sorted out by Freddie apologising and doing his best to explain that he was meaning to be sociable and not condescending.

Charlie took him on one side later and tried to explain that round here you didn't use a man's surname like that. It was too much like *'us and them,' 'Officers and O.R.'s'* – and in an area of few officers and masses of other ranks he had rubbed people up the wrong way.

By now though Freddie was accepted by almost everyone, and as he had been seen in the town with female companions, the 'gay' tag had virtually gone.

Charlie's full attention went back to what was being said.

'Solomons took me on and I jumped at the job. Jonty himself was too smooth for my taste – I simply didn't like him or trust him but beggars can't be choosers, as they say, so I finished up working for him. He was out a lot and anyway he had the two areas to keep an eye on so he needed a dogsbody – a 'gofer' is the term they use these days, I believe. I would go to the sales pitch or the repair shop – wherever he sent me – and basically did everything he threw at me. Rudimentary book-keeping, 'phone messages, pay a few bills, contact him if there was a possible sale – more or less everything. He didn't pay me much, but even so, I sometimes wondered why he needed to employ me at all. I was never over-busy and without my little contribution the place would have continued to run well enough. I was to find out quite soon why I was there.'

'I can see by the quizzical raising of the eyebrows – by the way it's very 'Roger Mooreish' Charlie – that the matter of handling books and cash puzzles you. Yes, Solomons knew all about my past. And, I was to find out soon enough – he knew all about my father and his position too. It was all in his master plan.'

'I knew that he knew a lot about me – the family and its money and my brush with the law. So these things were openly discussed between us – Solomons doing all the discussing. As far as I was concerned my family and previous history were my business.'

'So far I haven't told you about Solomons himself. He was regularly turned over by the police, but he was usually a move ahead of them. He was getting tips-off from the local gendarmerie and paid well for them. I know that for a fact. He'd done time at least twice before, but they wanted him again. His main scam was selling stolen vehicles. Top of the range models – Mercedes, Rollers, Jags, that sort of thing – were stolen and ended up with Solomons. He fitted them up with new plates and fresh papers and they were through the docks like a flash – out to his contact in the Middle East. He had other minor things going, but that was his main work. He sold a few ordinary cars from the site too, something that might help him to pass as a genuine car dealer. Something in the books for the tax man to see. He was a real bad sort. After a time working for him he began to act as if I was invisible and he made no real attempt to hide anything from me. I knew a lot about his dealings but he took it for granted that I would keep it all to myself. He was right, of course. Until now that is.'

'Even with all his interests, legal or not, he was greedy and always wanted more, and in me he thought he had a golden goose. He set me up for blackmail on the basis that my father would always bail me out to protect the family name and to keep it out of the newspapers. He was completely wrong. The old man wouldn't have raised a finger – noble family digit or not. I told Solomons this, but until he telephoned father and got the complete brush off he wouldn't accept it. Even after the phone call he still had hopes in that quarter.'

'What happened was this. There was a young woman there, Elsie, who cleaned his cars for him, made the tea and dusted round the office, that sort of thing. I saw her most days and found her pleasant enough even though she was always a little distant, not very bright and her thoughts were usually somewhere else. I scarcely knew her really.'

'Then one day we were in the office together and she started crying. She told me she was behind with her rent and the landlord was threatening her with eviction and possibly court action too. Somehow that didn't quite ring true, as it seemed rather futile to me as if the girl couldn't pay her rent then how could she pay a fine? When she told me that she was already on probation for shop-lifting I understood her problem. Any infringement of the terms she had to observe could end up with her going to prison.'

'Solomons came in at that moment and saw my arm round her shoulders and Elsie in tears. He began to bluster away about me taking advantage of a young woman and reporting me to the police. Obviously I told him it was all nonsense but his mind seemed made up on the matter. Then he checked the petty cash box – something that hadn't been opened that morning until then.'

'The outcome was that he then said he was twenty pounds short in the float and I'd taken it. Elsie was sobbing away continuously and Solomons was trying to look sympathetic. He said he would forget her part in the business if she wrote a statement saying that I had tried to sexually assault her, and that I'd taken the cash from the box to pay her.'

'Elsie jumped at this and wrote something out which Solomons locked away in his safe. He then let her go. She couldn't get out of the office quickly enough and stumbled on the stairs in her hurry.'

'It was all a set-up, of course and she was paid by him to stage the show. Solomons knew all about her probation and used it for his scheme by blackmailing her too. I told you he was a really nasty piece of work. He still has that paper and if he keeps his threat and uses it then I will be inside again for a spell, probably a long term this time.'

Freddie grimaced again as he sipped his bottle of cheap plonk and Charlie wondered why he didn't get Dougie to keep a decent red for him behind the bar. No-one else in the *Nag's Head* drank anything as exotic as a reasonable claret so his personal cache would be safe enough.

'That's my problem, Charlie. These days you're the closest thing I have to a friend I can turn to – so, to put it simply – can you advise me or see some way out of the jam I'm in? Any thoughts you might chip in with will be very, very welcome. I'm in a mess and need help.'

Charlie didn't know what to say. Until that evening he had known very little about Freddie and his life. To him he was little more than just one of the blokes in the pub – better educated and better spoken than the others but little more than a slight acquaintance. So Charlie did what came naturally to him and went to the bar for another pint along with Freddie's refill before responding.

'You've caught me on the hop here, Freddie. I haven't a clue what to say. I'd need to know much more about this Solomons fellow and his situation before I could even begin to think of offering a solution. I'd like to help though. He sounds like a real bad 'un who should be sorted out.'

'For instance. You know about his dealings in these stolen cars. Why don't you make it clear to him that what you have on him cancels out what he says he has on you? That might work. Then this Elsie girl. Why don't you try to trace her and get her to tell the truth to back up your story?'

Freddie was sipping his drink thoughtfully as he listened.

'Yes, I do probably have enough on him to tell the police a good story but Solomon has a contact with the local police he pays regularly, and anyway I have no written proof. It would be my word against his – and don't forget in their eyes I'm an old lag who has been helped out by a kind-hearted and compassionate employer. He just has to produce the paper from his safe and tell them I'm trying to wriggle my way out of the trouble I'm in. As for Elsie – she's terrified of him. He knows all the local gangsters and is a bit of a bully himself, so she knows that she would get a good hiding or even a face-slashing perhaps if she tried to retract her tale. And, don't forget, he could rig something that would break her probation. She could be inside in no time. He seems to hold all the cards.'

'Another option would be to move away from here and hope he doesn't track me down. If I did that I could end up looking over my shoulder all the time. I don't want to live like that. What I do want is to clear it up, once and for all.'

'I realise that what I've already paid him has gone – and I won't see any of it again – but I don't want Solomons to keep leeching off me every few months for the rest of my life. It's a tall order, I know, but you might have a thought or two that might help. He's a wicked man and should be in prison in my view.'

Charlie, who had been mainly a listener so far, spoke up.

'If we're talking about prison for wrongdoing then I'm with you, Freddie. I'm an old-fashioned 'small c' conservative man in my views. None of this Political Correctness and 'everyone's a victim' nonsense. And if we can rid the Met of a couple of bent coppers, then let's do that too. I have many friends in blue and I respect what they do. It's a hard job in the police and they deserve all the help they can get. I'd like us to write that into the ground rules if we do find there's something we find we can do.'

'We're agreed then, old boy. Let me put something to you, something that might be the basis of an idea and one that needs a man with your special sort of gifts to make it work. It's just the germ of an idea, that's all, but you might like it. OK Charlie? My thinking goes something like this.'

Charlie listened carefully to Freddie's little plan, liked it and suggested additions and improvements. The two became more animated as the discussion progressed and Charlie produced a small book and started to jot various things down in it. Freddie marked the occasion by having a fourth glass of wine before the two agreed to meet again the following evening to compare notes.

The final words of the evening came from Charlie. They were spoken in the manner of a man who was not drunk but was nearing the point when he soon could be. Inevitably some of the longer words did not come out as the speaker intended but neither of the men seemed aware of it.

‘In German there’s a word that we English don’t have that just about sums up the situation, Freddie. The word is ’schadenfreude’ ‘and it means getting pleasure from someone else’s discomfort. Having heard about your Mister Solomons a little bit of that might be called for, so let’s see if we are the ones to do it. Let’s drink to that.’

The two left the pub – Freddie feeling hazily happier than he had for some time – Charlie to go home and look for his personal phone book before he fell into bed.

TWO.

Before David Protheroe was born his father had two ambitions for him – that no son of his would ever go down the pit where his father had laboured for twenty three years and had the cough and the scarred body to show for every one of them, and that young Dai – his first son – would play rugby for Wales. Not in the pack where Protheroe Senior played as an journeyman back row forward for his local club, but in the glamorous backs to eventually become the latest in the distinguished list of great Welsh stand-off halves.

So when baby Dai was found to have his left leg shorter than the other and it later became clear that he would never be able to walk without a limp and running at any pace was not to be a realistic option, all of his father's hopes and plans became focussed on Idwal, born fourteen months after his brother and physically perfect. The unfortunate Dai also had a vivid birthmark scar on his right cheek that the medical people his father's Trades Union paid to examine the boy said could be made slightly less obvious, but would still blight him for his entire life. Also the boy had a slight turn in his right eye and was destined to be a short man even when full grown.

Shunned by a disappointed father and with his mother following his father's lead and merely tolerating her son, Dai was left to his own devices and became a nervous, introspective boy with no academic skills, and understandably enough, limited social graces. Uneasy in company he spoke only when he had to and was always embarrassed by a slight stammer that nature had added to his other defects. Nothing seemed to interest him particularly or hold his attention for long, and the only future anyone could see for him would be some moderately paid work above ground in the local pit. He seemed happiest when alone and that suited his family which by now had another boy and a girl to care for.

In the summer of his thirteenth year a small travelling fairground and circus arrived and set up its attractions down the valley at Cwern – about three miles from the Protheroe's home village. Dai found an old school satchel, filled a lemonade bottle with water, took a pork-pie from the fridge and an apple from the bowl on the kitchen table and trudged to the show. He spent hours there, carefully protecting and recounting his small hoard of coins. He went back home a changed boy with something in his life that for the first time had really taken his interest. Even his father, deep in his own preoccupations, could see a change in his son. His parents' enquiries as to the boy's day seemed to open a floodgate.

***

Dai had spent most of the day watching the knife-throwing of *'The Magnificent Modred'*. From what their son told them his absorbed watching of the knife-thrower as he practised on some ground behind the main tent had caught the man's eye, and he started to take some interest in the boy. He had been allowed to make a few tentative throws and appeared – according to what *'Modred'* had said to have a good eye and a genuine talent. Dai was going to return to the Circus the next day and see his new friend again. Pleased to see signs of a change in their unfortunate son his parents gave him a few shillings to add to his money and his mother made him some corned beef and brown sauce sandwiches to carry in his bag.

Dai had found his niche in life. He left school with a minimum of qualifications on the earliest date the law would allow and went off to join a small travelling circus that had a circuit around the English midlands. The job was found for him by his mentor *Modred* – whose real name of Arthur Bush had been dropped at the first opportunity as being not exotic enough for the glamorous trade he followed.

Dai was not bright but he was not stupid. He knew that all the glamour was superficial and that under all the glitzy costumes and glitter there were usually ordinary, hard-working people trying to make a living. All the performers were looking for that little something that would mark them as different in the eyes of the audiences who paid to see them.

He had been taken on to assist the show's big star '*Nero*' – an ageing and increasingly erratic thrower – who was the first to notice, then envy and finally grow to fear the skills of the younger man. As the circus's autocratic owner as well as its major attraction, *'Nero'* quickly decided that Dai had to go elsewhere.

Being unfairly dismissed by a rival jealous of his talent proved to be the turning point in Dai's short career. Always a hard worker he practiced even harder believing implicitly that his natural skills would soon be recognised and his efforts rewarded. Others were only too ready to employ the quiet young Welshman and by his late teens he had his first regular solo spot with a bigger touring show in the Greater London area and became *'Franco – The Masked Magician of the Blade'*.

As a man of only 5'4' with thick black curly hair and dark eyes the name he had finally decided upon for his career had something of the exotic about it to suit his gipsy-like appearance. The black mask he wore helped to hide the scar that had held him back previously and for a while his became an act seen regularly on television. In a striking black and silver outfit with black boots – the left one of which had a built-up heel that made his limp less obvious – his physical deficiencies were much less apparent. For a short period he was even something of a heartthrob and built up his own small bunch of female admirers. Within his circles they became known as *'Franco's Groupies'* and the name was even used in the *'Sun'* in a feature article that was cut out and became a much valued and regularly exhibited addition to Dai's wallet.

Technically he was superb, throwing knives of all sizes and styles, axes, and for a short time an occasional feature in the act was a competition between Franco and a former World Darts Champion with darts being thrown against Franco's knives. People who claimed to know about these things stated that Dai was easily the best knife-thrower currently performing and called him 'World Champion' and no serious challenges were made to take the unofficial title from him.

Speciality acts like Dai's inevitably have a limited time at the very top – that is if they ever do actually manage to get there. Dai had a few good years before his popularity began to wane. The public's reaction against circuses that had animal performers reduced attendances, and most people who saw Franco's act thought it entertaining but not enough to go to see more than once. He left the circus world and began to perform in night clubs with reasonable success and his future looked secure if not earth-shattering.

Then it all went wrong for Dai. A big television Charity Spectacular Show was arranged to raise money for an appeal for world-wide famine relief. Massive viewing figures were anticipated and many stars were very keen to be on the show – sadly, not always for altruistic reasons.

Dai saw it as a means of making a big come-back. He practiced like he had seldom practiced before – he had a new outfit and was convinced nothing could go wrong. Tonight was going to be his big night – even as low in the billing as he was.

Dave's stammer and fear of speaking were well known to his friends and associates but not, apparently, to the TV production team. Some young woman with a clipboard and purple hair told Dai just minutes before he was due to perform that a special award was to be made to him live in the show by a group of circus entertainers from the United States who had seen his act, and he would be expected to thank them with a little speech. *'Nothing too fancy – just how much you will treasure the Award – you know the sort of thing'.*

When, moments later, Dai went on to perform he was shaking like a leaf and in a terrible state. His act he had chosen for that evening was routine. *'The Exotic Juanita'* – actually Dai's wife Barbara – was lead to the vertical disc and her hands and feet were fastened to it. This part of the Act was controlled by a young and delightfully proportioned blonde assistant in a revealing blue satin dress. The wheel began to rotate at its carefully regulated speed and Franco simply had to throw his twelve knives as had done hundreds of times before. Most of the blades came to rest around the outer perimeter of the circle, far outside the line where they should have been. Three missed the wheel entirely and clattered to the rear of the set, two hit the disc but bounced out again to lie quivering on the studio floor. Just one was close to Barbara and she screamed loudly as it nicked her ear. She was still screaming when she was helped down from the wheel. All of this was seen and heard live and in gory close-up.

The repercussions for Dai were spectacularly bad. Barbara was convinced that the evening's show had been an attempt to murder her and have her replaced by the young assistant whom she fired on the spot, and Dai felt he was fortunate not to have a matching scar put on the other cheek by his irate wife who chased him round the studio with one of his knives in her hand. She did manage to knock out his two front teeth.

Her injury looked a lot worse than it really was but she insisted on being taken to hospital, and when she came back she told Dai that the next morning she was going to see about a divorce. The cameras had kept running throughout for what most people thought was the best live television they had seen for a long time.

Dai's career was finished. Millions of people had seen the fiasco as it happened and those who didn't would see the many screened repeats – all with mocking comments added. Over the next few days all of his bookings were cancelled and his diary was left completely blank.

THREE.

'You're wanted on the 'phone, boss. He don't sound happy.'

Jonty was upstairs in his office when the deep West Indian voice interrupted his day-dreaming. In his mind he was enjoying the hot sun of southern Spain, a long drink in his hand and with plans to go on the golf course soon. He didn't play, but when in Rome, etc, etc. He had a few old contacts in Spain and really he should be making plans very soon to look for a nice place out there. The money was ready, just waiting to be used. And the house over here – that was worth a tidy sum. He'd need a replacement for Miriam too. She was harmless enough and had been a good wife to him for years, but was so dull and predictable.

A younger woman would be better for his new life-style and image out there. It would cost him to see the old girl right and he'd get a lot of stick from the family, but it was his own life after all, and he planned to enjoy what years he had left. She'd become such a nag lately and had allowed herself to go to pieces – the weight was piling on her these days.

'What was that, Errol?'

'That Sean Connery fella' is callin'. He sounds niggled about sometin.'

To Jonty that was the last thing he wanted to hear. He picked up the telephone – quickly but reluctantly. His caller was a man he seldom wanted to speak to – and certainly not now.

'Hello, Angus. How are you? What can I do for you?'

Sean Connery was on the 'phone. Angus himself was the only person Jonty knew who seemed unaware of the remarkable similarity of his voice to the 007 actor, and no-one seemed willing, or foolhardy enough to tell him about it. Angus was an important man in his circle – very important and not a man to be taken lightly.

'Jonty, what kept you? Trying to avoid me are you?'

'You are in serious trouble. Very serious. You know I don't swear, Jonty, so I'll say no more than you're in very hot water. Mr. Gillespie is not pleased with you.'

Jonty knew better than to interrupt.

'You know, Jonty, we don't have any secrets from each other, do we? No, of course we don't. So why doesn't Mr. Gillespie know about your nice little earner on the side, eh? Why does he have to be told about it by someone else and not by you?'

Jonty could feel himself beginning to shake. This was seriously bad news.

He decided to speak to Angus who cut him off with a voice that oozed menace.

'Jonty, be quiet and listen to me.'

'We both know Mr. Gillespie is a fair man. A very fair man. He has no objections in the least to you or anyone else in our *'little group of associates'* who wants to make a few quid for himself. All very commendable – private enterprise and all that. He approves of private enterprise, does Mr. Gillespie. What he doesn't approve of, though, is theft. And theft it is when he doesn't get his share. You know what I'm talking about, don't you, Jonty?'

'He knows that you are in the blackmailing business on the side. We both know that you owe him a lot of money for his cut. Naturally enough, he wants his share. Soon. Very soon. So go into your piggy bank or under your mattress or wherever you keep your money, work out what you owe Mr. Gillespie and have it ready to be collected tomorrow morning.'

The tirade stopped but Jonty knew it would resume when Angus wanted it to.

'Because we're businessmen, Jonty, and time is money to us both I'll do you a favour. Don't waste time working out what you owe Mr. Gillespie, just write down on a piece of paper what I tell you to. Write it down now, Jonty. A pound sign followed by a figure two, then a nought, then a comma, then three more noughts.'

Jonty did as he was told and did not like what he saw on the pad in front of him.

'So let's just agree when we compare, Jonty – twenty thousand pounds you should have written down on your pad. You will see that the commission is considerably higher than normal but Mr. Gillespie has included an amount that he likes to call *'punitive damages'* because you have let him down. I know you understand what it means because I happen to know you're a *Telegraph* reader, Jonty.'

'Have it ready for tomorrow at eleven and make sure that bloke of yours has been sent off somewhere out of the way. I was going to send Tommy Craddock but instead you can meet another of our little team. Tommy's broken his hand on someone's jaw and so he's resting up at present. You'll like our new man. We call him Pancho – he doesn't speak any English, so don't waste your breath on trying to charm him. Just have the money ready for him when he calls. Just one thing about Pancho – he might leave you a message. If he does it will be short but certainly to the point.'

At this Angus began to laugh.

'Short and to the point, Jonty. You'll see what I mean tomorrow.'

The dry, high pitched laugh was from a man no-one had ever heard tell a joke or be amused by anyone else's, something that made what Solomons had just heard even more sinister. The telephone was put down at the other end leaving Jonty as uneasy as he could ever remember.

Craddock was a man who would give his old Granny a good hiding if Angus told him to and it was no good trying to resist him. Massive, muscled and thick – like a trained rottweiler. At least he wouldn't have him to face. Angus will be sending this Pancho character because he knows that realistically Jonty had no choice other than to pay up so muscle wouldn't be called for.

The real danger was Mr. Gillespie himself – *'The Big Man'*. No-one in his part of London dared cross him. It had been tried in the past and those who had dared to resist had vanished from the scene. Where they went to no-one really knew but there were plenty of suggestions – whispered gently of course. The currently popularly held view was part of the foundations for the M25 motorway. In earlier years the M1 to Luton had been favourite.

Solomons knew there was no point in trying to hide the truth. He'd been caught and had to settle up and put a brave face on it, even though the amount he was expected to hand over far exceeded the amount the blackmail had paid him so far. At least he still had the car scam working for him, a part of his business dealings that Gillespie knew all about. Thank God that he'd never tried to hide that from Gillespie and he was up to date with the *'commission'*, as Angus always called the creaming off of twenty percent of Jonty's profit. *'Commission'* or *'theft'* – Jonty was well aware he was in no position to argue.

Two things to do now. Make sure he had the money ready for tomorrow and try to work out how his venture into blackmailing had gone so badly wrong and how Angus had learned of his new sideline.

FOUR.

There are many animal sanctuaries in the South of England – some good, some less so, but all devoted to the welfare of the animals in their care. One of the most highly regarded and certainly one most often in the public eye was The Ashford House Animal Charity, near Reading. Started over thirty years ago in a rambling old house that was nearly decrepit, with some outbuildings that lacked roofs and several acres of rough arable land attached, it had become an impressive showpiece that was happy to open its doors to visitors who flocked in their hundreds most weeks. The Sanctuary had a dedicated staff that was proud to be linked with it and a reputation for animal care that was the envy of certain jealous rivals. But no-one aware of the Sanctuary's history would deny that without its founder and driving force, Gilbert Jeffries, the story of the last thirty years would have been completely different.

Jeffries was a run-of-the-mill actor who had a passion for animals. This passion had been his as long as he could remember and his choice of the acting profession was purely fortuitous. He was a big man – a massively built 6' 6' by his early twenties. He had drifted into boxing and was good enough to win regional titles. He played rugby and he was never clear in his own mind whether he played rugby to make himself fit for his exploits in the ring or whether the reverse was true.

In both sporting spheres he was decent performer, a tough competitor and a hard opponent to play against. Outside the ring or off the rugby field the term 'pussy cat' would have applied to him. He was a gentle, quietly spoken man who remained at the back of the crowd and always allowed others to lead. Except where his beloved animals were involved, where some inner demon took over and nothing was ever too much or no task was too hard for their needs.

He was seen one Saturday on a muddy rugby field by an individual who had fingers in many pies, one of which was film-making. He contacted Gilbert, offered him a screen test and the rest was history. The best known 'heavy' in British films was launched on his career.

Not that Gilbert was ever to be Oscar material. He would be the first to admit to his limitations in front of the camera. He was poor at remembering lines, had a gravelly voice that came over even in the best sound-systems as slightly muddied and he could never quite rid himself of a gentle Bristol accent that completely lacked any sense of menace. But he looked right for the parts – and that was what the men who made the films wanted.

None of these deficiencies stood in his way. His looks were his fortune. *'The ugliest man in Britain'* was the *Daily Mirror* verdict in one of his films and the term had stuck. Remarkably many women – and a lot of men – thought the term was unfair. He wasn't, in their view *'ugly'* – he simply had a lived-in, battered face. Years of boxing and rugby had left their scars. His nose had been broken several times and badly reset at least on one of these occasions while the cauliflower ears were simply a mark of his sporting career, as were the assorted scars around the eyes and cheekbones and missing teeth. Kind people simply said that the face of an unappealing child had become that of a rugged battered adult. They wanted him to look like a brutish gangster and his face obliged for him.

Whatever he had turned into the camera loved him. He would never in a million years be cast as a leading man with any romantic interest, but he was never short of work and many gangster films were built around him, even though nominally he was in a supporting role.

None of this worried Gilbert in the least. He knew his financial worth to the penny and he made sure that he was paid it in full. Then, as he began to have an extra degree of bargaining power he started to do what he became best known for. A fee would be agreed with the film-maker then Gilbert would simply add ten percent – money that was to go directly to his beloved Animal Sanctuary. Initially the studio would resist, then they realised that if they handled their reaction correctly and paid the extra that was being asked there would be good publicity for them and for the film concerned.

This became normal practice for Gilbert's fees and the results made the studios richer, and Gilbert's dream nearer to fruition. As he became older this well-known face appeared less in films but his Sanctuary consistently drew in more contributions than most did. The final accolade was a Knighthood that was awarded – not for services to films or acting but *'For services to Animal Welfare'* – a dedication that made Sir Gilbert a proud and very happy man.

FIVE.

Solomons followed Angus' instructions to the letter. He had the cash ready in a grey zip-up holdall and at twenty to eleven he sent Errol out to collect several parts for his cheaper cars on the lot – a journey he knew would take well over an hour. He sat in his big swivel chair and waited uneasily.

'Try to take your mind off things, Jonty. Cheer yourself up. Think of something pleasant.'

His eyes were drawn to the cork-faced notice board to his right on the wall opposite the door. Pinned to it was a calendar, a couple of official documents – a trading licence and a *Health and Safety at Work* notice that he used to impress his customers. What did often catch his customer's eyes – certainly the men almost invariably remarked on them after Jonty had casually, almost by accident, drawn their attention to the board – was a set of three coloured 8' x 10' prints. They featured just two men in each. Jonty was one, always beaming away at the man on his right and shaking hands as if they were bosom friends from years back. The pictures had cost him a couple of hundred pounds for the set. They were part of a fund-raising event with the beneficiary being a local children's charity and the three other men were members of the local football team.

But the footballers were special. The three were members of England's World Cup winning team and they were Geoff Hurst, Martin Peters and – in pride of place – the England captain, Bobby Moore. Jonty was not a football supporter but he knew the value of public relations. He told himself that when he went to Spain, they would be going with him even if most of everything else was left behind.

Thinking that adding something to them might seem a little too showy for their purpose; Jonty had deliberately left the three prints unframed but carefully pinned to the board exactly where he wanted them to be seen.

***

Jonty was nervous – and, as he admitted to himself later – he was frightened. The big doors downstairs were left open but his office door was shut. Jonty was determined not to be taken by surprise but even so he failed to hear anything until his door was opened silently and the man he had been told to call Pancho was standing in front of him.

Surprised would have understated what Jonty's feelings at that moment. Expecting a Tommy Craddock clone instead he saw this wizened little man with almost everything about him black. The silk shirt with long flapping sleeves and tassels, tight-fitting trousers, high-heeled shiny boots, black gloves and a black leather belt with unusual pouches that were closed by silver buttons. The blackness of his hair, dark eyes, strong signs of a five-o-clock shadow even at that time of the morning, ear-rings and that vivid scar on his right cheek. A strange creature whose slight stature did nothing to lessen the implied menace.

Jonty remembered that the man allegedly spoke no English but saw no reason not to try to humour him. Perhaps a little old-fashioned courtesy would help his cause with Angus. His *'Good morning, Mister Pancho'* went unanswered but the little man responded with what he clearly intended to be a smile of response that added to Jonty's unease when he saw the amalgam of gold fillings and gaps where teeth should have been. By now he was also aware that Pancho had eyes that never quite seemed to focus on him as they should and Jonty had difficulty in knowing exactly where he should look when he wanted to look the man in the eyes.

The two men, both still standing, looked at each other. Pancho held out his left hand and motioned towards the bag that lay on the floor next to the desk. Jonty handed it to him, Pancho checked the security of the fastenings, picked it up in his left hand and in three paces he was at the door.

Pancho turned and faced the office. Jonty was silhouetted against the weak sunlight that sometimes managed to get through his dirt-streaked windows at that time of the morning, and was watching the other man uneasily. The little man's next movements were almost too quick for the eyes to follow. Three silver buttons were undone and three knives appeared in his right hand – held by the points and with same watery sun reflecting off the shiny blades and jewelled handles.

With his left hand Pancho pointed towards the far end of the room. Instinctively Jonty looked there, to see three knives still quivering from the force of their entry into their targets. Their movement had been too quick for Solomons to follow. Each had found its target. In Jonty's three prized photographs the beaming man next to the star footballer had a knife in his heart.

Pancho went to the board, pulled out the blades, turned and was gone - as silently as he had arrived.

SIX.

Growing up in a particularly tough quarter of the east end, Jonty had to learn to fight to look after himself or life would have been impossible. He could still take or throw a punch if he needed to and was in reasonable physical condition, but as he became older and better off he saw how pointless that was and instead employed Errol to do it for him.

The West Indian was a decent enough mechanic, but no better than any one of a dozen Jonty could have hired. He was paid a little extra, in cash, for his looming physical presence, something that was very useful when a customer was being difficult about one of '*Jonty's Famous Deals – My Word is My Bond.*' And found the small print of the contract leaning too much in the dealer's favour. The big man usually did no more than be there and look menacing and the customer gave up, signed the papers and remembered to buy a car somewhere else another time.

Errol's presence downstairs and a locked door to his office were Jonty's two rules – laid down by himself and known to no-one but himself, just for the minimum security he needed to allow him to open his safe. On this occasion his preoccupations and the problems he had with Angus caused him to fall down on both.

He had his back to the door as it opened, turning quickly to see the two men who stood in front of him, filling the office as they did so. The faces weren't familiar but the bulk of the two was right for their errand. What did Angus want this time – the bastard? Think, Jonty, think. That Pancho weirdo has only been gone an hour or so.

Neither of the two men spoke for a minute or two.

'Mister Solomons? Mr. Jonty Solomons? We did knock – twice actually – but obviously you didn't hear us. Don't bother calling down for Frank Bruno – we sent him to the caff up the road. Gives us a better chance of having a quiet little chat, doesn't it, Jonty?'

The speaker was well over six feet tall and big with it. His manner of speaking was of a man used to power and a voice that carried authority – though the accent was from the North East and Jonty struggled to understand it all. He didn't hear many Geordies in Stratford East.

His colleague was a huge man – Jonty thought he was one of the biggest he'd ever seen. He might even qualify as one of the ugliest too with cauliflower ears and a nose that wasn't quite where it had started when its owner had been a baby and someone's pride and joy. He hadn't spoken yet and apart from going over to the safe and stopping Jonty from closing it, simply by standing in the way, his involvement so far had been minimal.

'He doesn't know us, Detective Sergeant Riddings. He knows all the chaps at the local nick – he has some very special chums down there, has Jonty – but he doesn't know us. I think we'd better introduce ourselves properly then to Mr. Solomons.'

Riddings stayed silent. The Geordie continued.

'I am Detective Chief Inspector Robson and I have already told you the name of my colleague. Show him your credentials Riddings. No, man, not like that. Leave your fly buttons alone.'

Then, in an aside to Solomons – 'He likes the old jokes best does my associate and I do try to keep my staff happy. It stops them from feeling too violent.'

Robson put back in his pocket the police warrant card he had waved at Jonty.

Solomons needed no reminder of the threat the two men were. They seemed harder and less tolerant than the local police he had had dealings with over the years – dealings that had become more expensive as time passed and his 'retainer' as they called it increased regularly – 'Just to keep up with inflation, Jonty. You know how it is these days.'

'Right then Jonty, no more levity. To business. Why don't we try to keep the civilities going and keep the unpleasantness to a minimum, shall we? You don't mind me calling you Jonty, do you? Good man, I thought you might agree.'

As far as Solomons was concerned he could have called him Buttercup and kissed him if he wanted to. Anything to keep him sweet and get rid of the two of them.

What Solomons didn't know was that Charlie was enjoying every minute of his act. Much of his portrayal came from an early eighties TV series in which he personally had been successful but the show had 'bombed' – a word he remembered the studio using at the time. Two things flashed into his mind – whether or not anyone else remembered *'On the beat'* – something he rather doubted – and if one of the mass of channels on *Sky* would repeat it. That would be a nice little earner, if it ever happened.

Concentrate Charlie – remember you're working.

'I see your safe is open. No doubt there's lots of private stuff in there that you don't want any Tom, Dick or Harry to see – or indeed, *'Frank and Ernest'* either. That reference to the *'well-known local schizophrenic'* is another little quip my associate enjoys – don't you,

Detective Sergeant? Just before you do lock it though, do you mind if we have a quick rummage.'

'You will have noticed, Mr. Solomons that both of us are house-trained and have worn gloves since we came into your office to avoid compromising any evidence we might touch, so you need have no fear of us leaving dirty finger marks all over the place. Shall we look then? After all, Jonty, you've nothing to hide in there, have you now?'

Riddings stood back and allowed Charlie to open the safe door wider and to look inside it.

'There is one thing we are looking for specifically today. Her Majesty's Government is most appreciative of your efforts in exporting vehicles but seems to lack the necessary paperwork to include the sales in the national figures – something we want to correct. I'm sure you wouldn't want your contributory part to the U K's economy going unrecognised. What you've done might even put you in the Honours List – all those big expensive motor cars. Much more than a humble copper could afford. I used to have an *Escort* but it was a bit small for a bloke like me so now it's a *Sierra*.'

'No Jonty, don't bother – our friend here will save you the trouble. You just sit there and tell us where everything is so that we find it quickly and can go very soon. '

'Shall we tell him where we go next, Detective Sergeant Riddings – or shall we keep our planned visit to the local nick to speak to a certain D.I. down there to ourselves? Oh, dear. Have I let it slip out? What a naughty policeman I am.'

Robson's apparently easy-going flippancy vanished in a moment.

'Come on Jonty – stop messing about. We know about the cars, the number changes, the shipping, everything in fact. We don't want to waste too much time on that – we leave the details to the office boys. We'll just take away any paperwork you have and then have our uniform people take you away. *'Carry on, Sergeant.'* (He likes that one too, Jonty.) Isn't my talkative colleague a wag?'

Robson's rapid mood changes were confusing Solomons. He was baffled by the man's jokes which fitted badly with the way things were looking for him. Clearly the police had more on him than he thought they had and their knowledge of his contacts down at the local station was not going to do him any good. Instead his years of bribery might go in his favour with the way the police were on corruption these days. He could always offer them something to stir the pot with. Slip in a name or two. Just a couple of bent coppers less. After all, nobody would miss them.

'Right, Solomons' – a change of name and another mood change for the increasingly confused Jonty – 'I'll just go through your safe and see what I can find before the serious stuff starts.' Keep an eye on him, George, try not to let him fight his way past you and force his way out through the door.'

Jonty had met many policemen in his time but never one like this. He simply didn't know quite how to deal with him. He'd probably a better chance trying to head-butt a brick wall than pushing his way past this non-speaking mountain of a sergeant.

'Mr. Robson. Chief Inspector. I know you probably believe you have something on me – perhaps you have – but can we do business?'

Charlie looked up from the safe. 'You mean you're attempting to bribe two police officers?'

'Certainly not. I wouldn't do anything like that. But I do have information that could be of value to you.'

Solomons looked hopefully at his tormenter. For a moment he felt the tension ease slightly. The next words confirmed his optimism. As usual, it was Robson who spoke.

'Jonty, my friend, sit down and make yourself comfortable. Just relax and say nothing till I've finished. Have a cigarette or something. Think about what you know and when I've gone through this lot here we'll have words. I'm so glad you want to co-operate.'

Jonty, feeling he should do anything that might ease the situation with the two, lit a cigarette – first taking care to offer the packet to the two massive figures who seemed to fill his office. Both men declined, Robson with a polite 'No thank you, Jonty' and Riddings with an equally courteous gesture without saying a word.

His offer to give them information seemed to have found the chink in their armour that Jonty wanted. In his mind he began to consider how much he could pass on to the two detectives and how much difference it would make to the outcome. Tactics? Should he allow what information he wanted to pass on about his various dealings with corrupt policemen dribble out over a period in an attempt to bargain, or tell them everything in one session?

His partial relief lasted just a moment.

'What's this, Jonty, this paper here?' Charlie showed it to Riddings, keeping an eye on Solomons who went white as he realised what it was.

'That looks to me like a statement alleging something serious about a young lady and the theft of some money. It's most definitely a police matter. What's it doing in your safe Jonty?'

Jonty mumbled something about *'keeping it safe for a friend before it was handed in to the police'*. It was the best excuse he could think of on the spur of the moment. Robson handed the paper to Riddings along with several others he had found and the huge man put them away in the cavernous pockets of his overcoat.

'Just three things before we leave you – for now that is. Firstly, we want the keys to the cars that match these papers we're taking away, and then I see there's your passport here in the safe. I think we should take that with us – just in case – and finally, and just for the record in advance of the full statement you will be called upon to give by somebody from the local cop-shop, we want you just to confirm verbally that the senior man on your payroll is D.I. Arthurton. Yes?'

Jonty nodded miserably.

'And Sergeant Morrison?'

Another nod. Jonty was feverishly considering possibilities to ease his position. It looked like another term inside – for a man nearing sixty that was a prospect he feared. He knew that some of his bargaining powers had already gone by confirming the names. His bargaining options had left him with just two things he could offer as a deal. Either Angus and Mr. Gillespie on a plate or making sure there was enough cast-iron evidence to properly put away some corrupt policemen – men who were hated and despised by police colleagues, the tax-paying public and by the criminal fraternity equally.

Grassing on Gillespie – the real *Mr. Big* in the local criminal set-up – would be just like signing his own death warrant and was not a serious option. In no way would any sane man consider doing that. No prison in the land would save him if Gillespie decided he wanted a grass disposed of. Jonty would probably be dead within a matter of days. The same applied to Angus. That left Arthurton and his side-kick. Now that he had confirmed their names to the two policemen he had nothing left to bargain with.

Arthurton was the only man he had told about Freddie Teddington and his family connections. Just three people knew about the blackmail. Freddie himself, Arthurton and Jonty. It could only have been Arthurton who told Gillespie prompting the call from Angus, a call that put him in the mess he was in now. They always said Gillespie had half the police force in London in his pocket and probably the local D.I. was on his payroll. So Arthurton was getting paid twice over. Nobody likes a bent copper. And we touch our forelock to them as they grab their bribes. Scum. Arthurton's the man to get. Hope he gets twenty years. Shop him properly, Jonty, and try to do yourself some good.

Back to earth with a bump.

That Geordie voice – mocking, teasing, wheedling.

'I can see you're thinking hard Jonty. What's that evil mind of yours telling you to say next? What is it? A plot to assassinate the Prime Minister or a coup at dawn on the seventeenth, eh? Do tell us, we both enjoy a good yarn, don't we, Riddings?'

The massive figure of Riddings still did not speak. Solomons found his silence more threatening than anything he could imagine the man saying.

'I have a diary.'

'Good man. I have one too. And what's special about this diary you have? Or is it that game we've all played as kids. Remember it Jonty? *'Show me yours and I'll show you mine'.'*

'My diary has dates, amounts and account numbers.'

Now he had done it. There was nothing in reserve to bargain with.

‘Well done, Jonty. They say confession is good for the soul. Hand it over then and show me.’

Jonty did as he was told. Robson had a quick look at the diary’s contents, asked for clarification on one matter and the book disappeared into Riddings pocket.

‘Thank you for your time, Jonty. Some of our colleagues will be in touch very soon. Just wait for them and don’t do anything foolish, will you? We’re leaving a couple of plain clothes officers outside to make sure those two big saloons aren’t touched – they are police evidence now so give your man the rest of the day off when he turns up. You won’t see my two chaps even if you look for them – they’re very good at hiding. They’ve left their big, squeaky boots at home today. Just stay in the building, there’s a good chap.’

Riddings still hadn’t spoken when the two left. They took with them a leather case from the safe with over forty thousand pounds in cash – mostly in large denomination banknotes.

Solomons was arrested two hours later by officers he did not know and taken to a police station he did not recognise from the inside.

SEVEN.

They chose an hotel in Solihull for the celebration, handy for the four of them and conveniently near the M6. With rooms booked for an overnight stay each was able to drink as much as he chose – Freddie set a new personal record that night with five glasses of a wine much better than *The Nag's Head* had in its cellar.

Dai admitted he had revelled in the role of *'Pancho'*. If he had missed with one or two of his three throws – so what, there was no audience. He'd no lines to remember and just had to do what he was best at. With no pressure he'd enjoyed the morning's work and a lot of his confidence had come back. Among friends the apparently taciturn semi-recluse with a stammer was good company and had a fund of stories.

The little Welshman told them of his early life and how happy he was now that he and Ingrid – his latest assistant – were 'an item.' Some studio in America wanted him to feature in a western and he'd always believed that if he'd been around in the days of the silent films, well – *'Pancho'* might have become a big star.

***

Gilbert admitted that any payment for his half-hour's work was 'money for jam'.

'I simply had to stand there, listen to what Charlie said and follow any cues as to when to move and when to stand still. As for looking menacing – well, just look at me. I'm 90% there, aren't I? Not that I'll turn the fee down, of course – and very generous too, thank you, Freddie – and you all know where it's going.'

All Gilbert's props were the real thing. A genuine warrant card, handcuffs, police notebooks – all used in various films and 'They never came and asked me for them back after we'd finished. They can have them anytime – all they have to do is make a donation to the Sanctuary.'

***

Freddie naturally was delighted. He had his money back and even after generous payments to the team there were a few thousand pounds in his pocket he thought had gone for good. In fact he had come out with a profit. He felt that he had done little to recover his own money – but the others reminded him that he had approached Charlie and told him of the problem and sowed the seeds of the plan that Charlie worked on. *'DCI Robson'* pointed out that without Freddie's personal courage in coming forward and by owning up to the *'little problem'* in his life none of the affair would have happened. Anyway hadn't he made some more good friends because of what had happened? Freddie was a happy man that evening, content with his lot and enjoying their company and his wine. What was that German word again Charlie?

***

The happiest of them all was Charlie. Most of the scheme had been his and he had made use of what skills he'd learned over the years. His ego had been given a boost when some of his bounce and confidence was starting to drain away – his plan seemed to have helped a friend's flagging career, and he'd made a few quid. Not bad for an ageing thespian. He admitted to the others that at times he had thought of adding a bit off the cuff but was glad after he'd stuck to the plan. Even so he had been tempted. It just shows you what people can do when they try.

***

Charlie was well away by the time he came up with his big idea – a strategy for their futures.

‘Here’s a thought for the three of us. Suppose Gilbert sits on a stool with Dai on his lap and his hand up Dai’s back. There’s a screen behind and I go behind that. Gilbert is the ventriloquist, Dai is the dummy and I do the voices. That would work wouldn’t it? Folks would love it. The ugliest vent with the ugliest dummy in the business talking like Basil Fawlty. At least it would be different.’

At this point Dai began to repeat the phrase *‘A gottle o’geer, a gottle o’geer’*, giving the victory sign, waving a small cigar in his other hand and attempting an impersonation of his own. The impression was so bad that the others insisted on the Welshman buying a round of drinks to compensate.

Within minutes Charlie and Dai were both fast asleep. It needed all of Gilbert’s strength, with Freddie fluttering around like a sparrow with an injured fledgling trying to help, to carry Charlie up to his room. On the second trip upstairs Dai was simply tucked under Gilbert’s arm and carried like a rag doll. All four slept the deep and undisturbed sleep that comes after a job well done.

EIGHT.

Jonty was sixty on the second of the month – a Tuesday. He had slept badly the night before, and a simmering dispute with the big Glaswegian 'Razor' Devlin made him uneasy. He knew that there was no way to avoid the other man and that the matter had to be settled very soon – probably later that same day. There were three letters for him and after a quick glance he left the one with familiar handwriting to be opened last.

***

The first letter had a London postmark. It was written in pencil on cheap lined paper.

Dear Mr. Solomons,

This is from Elsie Mr. Solomons. Elsie what used to kleen your office for you. I want to thank you for your cheqk and the kind thorts you sent me through Freddey. I was very suprisd when it came. £500 is very welcome. Freddey sed that the paper that you asked me to sin has now been ripped up something that I am very glad about and greatfull for. Freddey was always very kind to me and I never did like what you did to him. I hope you dont find prison to hard.

Elsie Walters (Miss)

***

Jonty didn't like the second letter either. Animals had never been a part of his life and unless there was something in it for him, Jonty turned a deaf ear to charity appeals. So receiving a hand-written letter from the Hon. Treasurer of The Ashford House Animal Charity thanking Mr. Jonathan Solomons for a generous donation of £2000 did not please him.

***

The third letter did not contain the card that Jonty expected. Inside were two sheets of pale blue, delicately scented paper closely written in an immaculate hand with backward sloping script.

'Dear Jonty,

I don't know your new official address but I hope that sending this letter to Her Majesty's Prison, Wormwood Scrubs will find you.

By the time you receive this I will be in Spain – somewhere I always fancied but which never seemed to appeal to you for some reason. That's just another thing we didn't share.

Good villas don't come cheap but with everything in England being in my name I managed to raise the money with enough left over to live on quite comfortably when I'm out there. The house sale – I included the furniture – made a good price and the crazy way house prices have shot up in London worked out well for me. I have taken most of the cash but left you some that I put into your own personal account. Not much, but there again you probably won't need much for another eight years, or so I'm led to believe. I expect you still have some money hidden away that I don't know about.

I have started the ball rolling for a divorce. It makes sense doesn't it? I discussed what I'm doing with the children and they all approve and they haven't any plans to visit you.

I bumped into Naomi (Greengross) the other day and she seemed very envious of me. My slimming regime has worked well and I've lost well over a stone – from the right places too. She used a word that you, as a crossword man, will know – 'svelte'. What a lovely word that is. I had to look it up but I'm glad I did. It was worth it. It does wonders for the self-esteem. All I needed was a reason to start slimming, and you going gave me that reason.

As much as anything I think she was rather jealous of my companion. You haven't met Mike, but he's twenty-four, blonde, dishy (Naomi said she wants one like him too) and built like a Greek god. Not Jewish by the way. Mike will be going to Spain with me.

If you have anything to contact me about, please do it through our Solicitors. They have been instructed not to release my new address. You should be hearing from them soon anyway.

Miriam.

PS. Guess who I ran into recently when I was doing some shopping in Harrods? An ex-employee of yours – Freddie. Remember Freddie? Well, he's now Lord Chessington (like the Zoo). His father died so he inherited the lot. It sounds as if he's a very wealthy man now. You should have kept in with him. His Lordship said if I contacted you I was to pass on a message – something about two mutual friends – 'very big friends' I was to say – and 'the little darts player' were pleased the way things turned out, and to say 'Didn't Sean make a good impression?' He was quite specific about the wording and said you would understand.'

Jonty read through the letter a second time – still not quite believing what he saw.

NINE.

A bad day became even worse as 'Snouty' Green popped his head round the open door.

'Mr. Devlin wants to see you Jonty – 'very soon' he said. I shouldn't keep him waiting if I was you. He's got Big Fergie and McKinnon with him and they don't look happy. They're in the showers.'

Solomons shrugged his shoulders. He took off his reading glasses and put them into a case and put the case under his pillow.

'Don't bother reporting back to him, Snouty. I'll find them. I know what it's about. I'm the birthday boy today and they have something special arranged for me.'

MAGIC MOMENTS.

(Published in *Winamop.* July 2012)

'Arbuthnot. What a name to christen anyone with. Something about millstones and necks comes to mind. To this day I've never forgiven my father for it. He's gone now but he did tell me that I was named after his father's brother who lived over in the States. All because his Uncle Art, as he was called, had made pots of money after emigrating, and dad hoped some of it would come my way after this rich great-uncle kicked the bucket. It didn't and so I was stuck with a name I always hated. Fortunately for me, when I took up acting I could do something about it, and as long as *Equity*, our actor's union, didn't have an identical moniker on their list, I could be who I wanted to be. The surname of Armstrong I could live with but I changed it anyway. So *Peter Tyndale* was born. And I've never regretted my choice. It's been good for me.'

'Not that it's an easy profession to be in. There are always far more people looking for work than there are jobs available. Making films, T.V. or stage work, the same thing applies. It's an exceptional actor or actress who is always busy. And when you're not – well.'

'*'Resting'* we call it in the profession. To you and to most other people it's being out of work, but we actors are a funny lot – and proud with it. Some of us won't always face facts and like to hide the truth from ourselves. Then, as you move up the ladder the terminology changes – like me, for instance. Now that I'm a name, a face people know, I don't *'rest'* – at my level we're *'between jobs'* or *'reading up for my next film'*. The truth is, it all boils down to the same thing – you're unemployed.'

‘Well, back in my earlier days, before you were born even, I was a poor, down-trodden bit player taking any jobs that came along. Telly commercials with me playing the bloke in the defensive wall in front of the goalkeeper who has the football kicked at his vitals; one of the queue who gets splashed when the bus comes along; the guy reading the paper whose face you don’t see; the fourth frog from the right in the second row – you grabbed anything that came along. It didn’t matter whether you moved or not, or whether you spoke a line – so long as you got full union rate and a cheque out of it – that was all that mattered.

‘It was never enough to live on properly so when Marcus Rifkin – he was my agent at the time just as he still is – Marcus found me a few days work at Hummages on Oxford Street. I nearly took his hand off I was so keen. Indoors, in the warm, a guaranteed number of days work, use of the staff canteen with subsidised meals and a morning coffee break. Wow! That was Heaven on earth to me in those days.’

‘Witchcraft was big that year. Disney had released *‘The White Witch and the Magic Pearl’* and it was the hit of the season with the kids. Wonderful animation I recall. Being Disney they merchandised the film like only they can, and the toy shops were packed out with bits and pieces connected with it. You didn’t seem to be able to go anywhere or switch on the telly without being reminded of the film.’

‘Well, naturally all the big London stores were in on the act and everywhere you looked people seemed to be making money out of the Black Arts – except that being Disney there was nothing nasty anywhere. Even the old witches on the broomsticks were loveable old ladies like everybody’s idea of the perfect granny. You know how sentimental the Yanks are – All-American moms and apple-pie, that sort of thing.’

'The film was launched in the UK to coincide with Halloween and the plan was for the sales campaign to carry on and overlap the Christmas period. Naturally enough Hummages wanted to put on something that would allow them to get their share of the action. In fact the store had decided to follow the same pattern they used for the Christmas Grotto, but with an extra area in the basement dedicated to the Witches and Magic theme.'

'Obviously instead of Father Christmas they substituted Witches, Warlocks and Wizards – except that there weren't any warlocks, the men were witches – with a solitary Wizard in there too. The reasoning was that the Disney people thought that Warlock wasn't a word that the public would recognise, so male and female alike were referred to as Witches. A sort of 'dumbing down' – at least that's the way some of the stuffier papers saw it.'

'The area was festooned with cobwebs, and spiders' webs were trailing all over the place, there was a massive imitation fireplace with a huge cauldron simmering away, a broomstick in the corner of the hearth and a stuffed black cat with yellow eyes that purred and miaowed – really lifelike I remember. It was all quite impressive – or at least the kids seemed to like it. Enough to make the parents spend their money and, after all, that was the point of the exercise anyway.'

'There was a little bit of resistance from people in one of the Churches who felt that the children were being exposed to malign influences, but they represented a minority and inevitably they were on a loser. There was no way that these days they could compete with Mammon and expect to come out on top. It was like a vegetarian take-away with premises next door to McDonalds.'

‘Where I fitted in was that they put me into a wizard’s outfit with a red cloak patterned all over in symbols and astronomical signs and things, and a big pointy hat that was covered in glittery stars. In those days there was less of me than there is now and that made me ideal for the part. As the Wizard I was the big cheese there, and expected to ponce around and basically be centre stage most of the time. With an ego like mine I was in my element. Somebody said I looked a bit like a young Basil Rathbone.’

‘No? You youngsters. No soul at all. You look blank. Never heard of Basil Rathbone? He’s part of our nation’s cultural heritage. Like Bruce Forsyth’s ‘cuddly toy’ and the *‘Carry On’* films. If you watch enough telly late at night or in the afternoons, you’ll run across him sooner or later. An actor from way back in the old black and white days – dark, lean and best known for his *‘Sherlock Holmes’*. Look under the deerstalker in *‘Hound of the Baskervilles’* and you’ll see him.’

‘They also gave me a wand that they told me to wave about a bit and ‘*make some magic’*. Fortunately for me the store had laid on a couple of places in the area where magic actually did appear to happen. An elaborate wave of the stick with my right hand well away from my left to distract as I pressed a hidden button, caused an illuminated miniature fountain to start gently spurting water that they had already treated with coloured crystals or something. The kids seem to be impressed though some of the parents weren’t. Then the same sort of thing was done with coloured lights – hidden button, wave my wand and say the magic word.’

‘There were also places where smoke would appear on cue. They would have used sparklers but the Health and Safety people wouldn’t allow that inside the building – they felt that the fire risk was too great.

They had told me to say 'URAMBALI' every time I did a 'magic' trick. Under my breath I sometimes did say 'Abracadabra' but the word they heard me use was a big part of the film and the sales pitch to sell to the children and had to be used a lot.'

'By the end of Day Two in the store I was bored out of my mind. The Supervisor already had his eye on me – '*my attitude was wrong*,' he said. He also told me that he had heard me *'HoHoHo-ing'* to myself. I'd been trying my best lines on a couple of the younger mums but hadn't got very far. Then I started to try a few basic conjuring tricks I remembered from my schooldays. Mister Gullick, the 'Mister' seemed to matter a lot to him – seemed to find this acceptable until he accused me of trying to show a couple of spotty schoolboys how to *'Find the Lady'* – and this wasn't even for money.'

'Well, there I was on a yellow card with every likelihood of the red one following and I would be out on the cold, wet streets with no money coming in and Christmas getting closer by the day. So, on the morning of the third day I was on my best behaviour. It wasn't easy, but I stuck at it. Then I saw this beautiful lady and the day changed. Blonde hair, the loveliest smile you've ever seen and a figure you would die for. She was gorgeous.'

'Naturally I started to chat her up – Gullick was on his break fortunately – and felt I was getting somewhere. She bought something for her little boy and I had managed to charm a phone number out of her and was as happy as a sandboy. I was able to find out what the form-fillers would call her 'marital status':– she was divorced. Sad for her but it suited me. Then Gullick returned and was all smarmy and creepy to the woman, but I knew he was watching me. Probably it was jealousy. He really fancied himself and when there was no-one about he was trying it on with the girls in the Grotto. They hated him but they had jobs to protect so they had to be very careful how they turned him down.'

'Gullick's return ended the lovely atmosphere and the woman decided it was time for them to go. I knew we were going to meet again soon, so – mainly for the child's sake – I made a big thing of seeing them to the way out. The boy was as serious as only little boys can be – completely impassive all the time. Not sulking or anything but his expression never changed, even though I knew very well he was taking it all in and not missing a trick. (Sorry about that, the pun wasn't planned).'

'For years now I've had a little mannerism. A snap of my fingers at automatic doors, pretend they open at my command – it was just something I did. And still do it to this day. Just simply a personal thing. Harmless fun. Well, the entrance and exit for the Grotto was through a pair of heavy glass doors that opened in the middle when the magic eye thing was activated, so when they were about to leave I went to the doors. I didn't snap my fingers but waved the wand and said the magic word *'URAMBALI'*– loudly just as I was expected to do. Somebody up there must have liked me that day for the timing was right – absolutely spot-on to the fraction of the second. The doors swished open and I was rewarded by a lovely beaming smile from the child – a smile that would have tugged at the heart-strings of old King Herod himself.'

'I bowed very low, down as close to the boy as I could and gave him the wand. I say gave him – in fact it was a near formal presentation that I felt was needed for this beautiful, serious child. I offered my hand to him – he reached up and shook mine in return in a grown-up, dignified way. It was almost like the Queen awarding an honour in

Buckingham Palace. The two of them left and I knew something important had happened in my life.'

'After they had gone out of my sight I turned to see Gullick watching me.'

'*'That was not your property to give away, Tyndale. It belonged to Hummage's. Its cost will be charged to you and deducted from your pay. You have already had a warning – I personally put it on your record card. Consider yourself dismissed and finish when the store closes this evening. Collect your wages before you leave.'* He went off to the internal telephone – presumably to arrange the financial side of things and whatever other details needed to be sorted with the office.'

'I didn't bother arguing with him. I knew that I wouldn't have won and it simply wasn't worth it. There are Gullick's everywhere. They're just part of Life's Rich Tapestry.'

'Still – all's well that ends well so they say. Two days later I auditioned for a part in a film – just a little part but it was big enough to give me the big breakthrough that put me where I am now.'

'Funnily enough when my book came out a year or two later – I put my name to, even though I actually wrote about two paragraphs in it with a ghost writer doing the rest – they wanted me to do a book-signing thing at Hummages. I saw Gullick that day.'

'Apparently one of the girls had eventually complained about his pestering her, and then the others joined in to support her. I saw one of them when I went there with the book and she told me how the store management had handled it. Gullick was demoted and told that it would be a police matter if it happened again. At least it left the worm with a job of sorts. I saw him with a bucket and mop cleaning in the gents where someone had been sick. He recognised me too – that was a little something I enjoyed.'

'And, yes, I did see the lovely lady again. The little boy is Michael, your brother – and that's how your mother and I met. So your existence in this world is partly down to old Walt Disney himself. How many people do you know who can say that?'

'So, no 'Arbuthnot' for you to hide from, my boy. Your mother and I both agreed on that. And that's why you're who you are, young Walter.'

GRANDAD'S OLD FLAME.

(Published in *Delivered.* November 2010.)

I usually see grandad once a week. Tuesdays and Thursdays are my training nights so they're spoken for, and weekends are strictly mine, so this latest time when I called round it was a Monday. I like the old chap. It doesn't feel like a duty call just to keep in touch – it's something I really enjoy. Though he's nearly in his eighties, he still has his marbles, apart from going a bit deaf and forgetting things now and then. He can be a bit cranky as well, but on his own since gran died I suppose it's understandable.

As well as doing the odd job around the place for him I learn a bit too. Over the last year or two I've developed an interest in genealogy and he tells me a lot about the family and the old days. The *'new man'* hadn't been invented back then, so apart from making tea and toast and putting something between slices of bread, he's hopeless in the kitchen. Mum pops round when she can and makes him a meal and cleans up a bit for him, but living on sandwiches, bought-in pies for microwaving and the occasional fish and chips from round the corner doesn't seem to worry him, and it lets him keep his pride and independence.

Anyroad, I went round that evening and just let him go on a bit. Being on his own most of the time he likes an audience when he has one, so I just sit back and listen. He talks about football, cricket, the rubbish on television he complains about but still watches, Council Tax, the cost of living, Political Correctness and, of course, *'the clowns down in Whitehall'* as he alls them. So I gave him his head for the usual few minutes and then threw my bombshell at him.

'I ran into an old flame of yours from way back at the weekend, grandad.'

There was nothing wrong with his hearing that day. He was in full flow but that stopped him.

'Who're you kidding, lad? That's a very select group of young women you're talking about, but none of 'em round here. You've got it wrong. Not my old stomping ground, you know that. Go on then. Tell your tale.'

'No, this is straight-up. You know I'm seeing a girl over in Elgerton? – Tracey, Tracey Goodall – '

'–Don't know any Goodall's. Never knew any Goodall's.'

'Let me finish, granddad. Well, the other day over there I was talking to her mum and for the first time I met her gran. She knew I was called Martin but didn't know my surname, so she asked me what it was. When I told her it was Dilloway it seemed to ring a bell, so she asked if we were from round here.'

'So I told her that you and gran had moved here to Manton from Lancashire years ago. She wanted to know exactly where from and first names – that sort of thing. As soon as I told her you were Stephen, and Gran had been Iris, she reacted and said that you and she had had a date – back when the Kaiser was alive.'

'Cheeky young sod. Did she really say that?'

'No, Granddad. It's just me – don't forget I inherited your sense of humour.'

'You're trying to wind me up, aren't you? What's her name then?'

'Alice Warren.'

'Don't know any Alice Warren – but I'll bet you fifty pee that her husband was called Bunny.'

‘She says you’ll remember her as Alice Carfoot.’

Granddad went quiet.

‘Well I never. Yes, I do remember an Alice Carfoot but never as a girl friend in the way you mean it. That’s remarkable. Yes, we did have date once. D’y know Martin, that was over sixty years since? Nearly three of your lifetimes. Shortish girl, thin face, wore specs, blonde – I think.’

‘Grey now and a bit plump. Come on then Granddad. Tell me all about your wicked past.’

‘Nice little story if I can remember it. One that makes your old granddad look a bit foolish but that’s nothing new. Go and put the kettle on and I’ll try an’ get the old memory working for you.’ Three sugars but no milk. It must be in the genes as dad and me both drink our tea that way – just as the old boy likes his.

‘I’ll tell you something, lad. Nobody, and I really mean nobody – knows this story. I’ve never told a soul about it so don’t go blabbing off to your father. Let’s keep it our little secret. O.K?’

‘As best as I can remember I would have been about fourteen – maybe going on fifteen. At that age in those days the lads stayed together as a gang and so did the girls in their own huddle, and the idea of going around together as a mixed group that seems to be the way nowadays was something that never happened then. Obviously we were aware of girls and many of our evenings seemed to be spent looking at each other – the boys posing, boasting and generally showing off, and the girls giggling and whispering away to each other like they do. There was no pairing off or anything like that – that was a year or two off. At the ages we were we back in those days wouldn’t have known what to do anyway. We were all so innocent. Your generation just wouldn't believe how it was back then.'

'Alice Carfoot was simply one of the girls. I just about knew her name and the school she went to and that was all. I remember she was especially pally with a Marjorie James who years later married Dave, one of the lads.'

'Well, about then there was a dance coming up down in the Youth Club in Peter Street. It wasn't a proper dance with a band; it was something put on with records and things. All on 78's in those days. You probably won't even remember them. Black, heavy, scratchy as hell and they broke as soon as you looked at them. For all of us lads it was the first ever dance we'd ever been to. Some of the girls might have been able to dance but none of our lot could. Some years later we all could dance after proper lessons became the thing, and the local Co-op Hall on Saturdays became the highlight of the week, but that was for the future. Tickets were about sixpence each in old money (that's two and a half pee to you), and we all finished up going. Inevitably there was a lot of nudging, cajoling and 'dares' but not one of us danced a single dance that night. Most of the time it was us on one side and the girls on the other just looking across the room at each other. Some of the lads we knew but weren't in our lot spent the evening in one corner playing cards. Anyway, that was the night my date with Alice was arranged.'

'I'd never made any moves towards this particular girl, or any of 'em if it came to that, but somehow or other the girls told the other lads that this Alice had said *'she liked me'* and that was enough. Between them they all fixed it so that this girl I didn't know and me were to meet up the following Friday evening – just the two of us – on a 'date.' It was one of those silly things when I was stuck in a situation I didn't want and couldn't wriggle out of without looking stupid in front of everyone else. And pride and not losing face at that age was very important – as I'm sure you can remember.'

'So Friday evening came – it was a dark night, October or November, something like that, and I was to go out on my own and meet a girl for the very first time. One I barely knew, didn't remember ever speaking to and would have struggled to recognise when she wasn't with all the others. And it was pouring down – and that's putting it politely. As well as that I hadn't a clue what was expected of me. Me, Stephen Dilloway, at fourteen – never been kissed – and certainly never out with a girl!'

'What had been arranged by everyone else for us was that we were to meet at the park gates at seven. Now the old Recreation Ground was at the bottom of our road so it was handy enough for me – no more than a hundred yards or so from our front door – but where Alice lived I hadn't a clue except that it must have been somewhere in the area. At that age unless I was with my pals I normally stayed at home in the evenings, and as it was so wet my parents thought I was barmy when I said I was off out. By the way for you students of the Dark Ages – staying in then meant listening to the wireless, homework or reading – there was no telly back then. Just think about that lad.'

'My folks quizzed me about it and looked at each other thinking they'd spawned an idiot son, but I made up some story about seeing Dave and Pete and perhaps going round to one of their houses, something like that. They didn't believe me but I don't think for a moment they would have thought a girl was involved – not for their little Stephen at the age he was. Bit of a goody-goody I was then, I'm ashamed to say.'

So, there was I at the big gates of the park about ten minutes early, standing in the rain like a prat, already wet through and wondering what I was expected to do when the girl turned up. I had two or three bob in my pocket but there was nowhere at that time of evening to go out of the wet – no café or anything like that except perhaps in the town centre and that was too far away to consider in weather like that. I suppose we could have gone to the pictures but it would have had to be the second house and the show would have ended too late for me to get home at a reasonable time, never mind what her parents would say about their daughter staying out till well after ten.

I knew enough of the basics of dating etiquette to be aware of just two things — that the gentleman walked on the outside of the pavement, and that he should always see the lady home. The only thing I could come up with would be to go and sit in the seats at the pavilion down near the bowling greens. At least we wouldn't be in the wet there.'

'I didn't have a watch, but I could hear Beecham's clock striking and by about quarter past I was wet, cold, miserable and this girl hadn't turned up and the rain seemed to be getting heavier by the minute. By seven-thirty I'd reached desperation point and went down to the pavilion and sat in the dark down there wondering what to do.'

'I went home and got there just after eight, and my mother fussed over me for ages helping me to dry off, put paper in my shoes and hang my school mac up near the fire. Mam had some old-fashioned ideas – one of which was that going out with wet hair after a bath would give you a cold, so you can perhaps imagine how she was about her darling, saturated boy. I went to bed early that night, from choice, and once I was warm, dry and snug, everything was fine.'

‘There was still the matter of what to tell the other lads. Naturally they wanted to hear how the date had gone. I simply decided to brazen it out and as far as they were concerned I had met this girl and everything was fine. Of course there were questions which I simply either ignored or invented answers to, so if they asked me – the main question being ‘Was I going to take her out again?’ I simply said that ‘We hadn’t decided and were thinking about it’. You have to remember, Steve, the other lads were as naïve as I was about girls then. This was all back in the middle-ages.’

‘I did see her again on the next night – the Saturday – and as usual she was just one in the crowd of girls. I didn’t speak to her directly – and in fact, to this day I have never spoken to her face to face. You probably find that hard to believe about an ‘old girl friend’ but it’s true.’

‘One of her friends slipped me a note – nudge, nudge, giggle, giggle, as they do at that age – and when I read what Alice had written she’d done the sensible thing and not turned up because of the rain. But she did say that as far as all her pals were concerned she’d told them we’d met as arranged and everything had been great.’

‘So Alice had kidded her friends along just as I had with my pals. She was trying to save face with her lot – just as I was with mine. And that was something it took me quite a while to realise – at first I was conceited enough to think that what she’d done she did for me. But even if I got her motives wrong, it did stop me looking as big a fool as I felt at the time. After all – she could have just said that she’d been stood up. That she turned up and I didn’t. If she’d said that, well you can imagine how I would have looked. She didn’t, but her bit of fibbing and mine meshed and the way they fitted together suited us both.’

'I scribbled a note and slipped it back to her just saying that I hadn't turned up either, and told her what I'd said to the lads. No-one else was ever the wiser. So even Alice doesn't know what actually happened – just what I told her. As far as she's concerned I never turned up. There's an old saying that goes like this: *'There's only me an' thee who knows, lad, and when I get mi clogs on there'll only be thee.'* So remember young Marty, Mum's the word.'

'So, there's a girl I didn't know back then and haven't seen since the late nineteen-forties, but I still remember something she did. It was for herself really, but it did me a good turn too. Give her my regards when you see her again, lad. No, make it sincere regards, I owe her that much.'

'There's more to it than that, Grandad. Mrs. Warren – Alice – wants to meet you sometime to talk over old times, she says. She's on her own now, so you'd better look out. If you do need some protection from the Merry Widow – I can always be a chaperon. She might even suggest a walk in the park on a wet Friday night? If she does and you want someone to ride shotgun – well, just give me a shout.'

‘DON’T COME TILL WE CALL YOU.’

(Published in *Winamop*. January 2014)

That must have been the moment I died. Nobody’s head hitting a motorway bridge like that could have survived. I remember the seatbelt snapping, my body going through the windscreen, pieces of glass everywhere in my face, then pain like nothing I’d ever felt before.

A void – silent, black and infinite.

In a hazy fashion I began to hear something I didn’t know and couldn’t recognise. I felt my head and body and looked around – everything seemed intact and working – except my watch. It had stopped at 9.58.13.

A man I didn't know and couldn't understand was talking to me.

As my mind cleared I began to make some sort of sense of what he was saying.

‘What's your number? Where's your docket?’

He was a tubby little man, five feet or just over, aged about sixty. Pale faced with a large nose, with false teeth that were either not his own or were his but the wrong size, so when he spoke it was with a clacking noise. What hair was left was grey and combed straight across from below his left ear and plastered down to make the most of what remained, in the way that Bobby Charlton used to. Not an attractive person to be accosted by when you haven’t a clue where you are or even what time it is.

He was holding a clipboard, and in his top pocket I could see a selection of coloured pens and a bleeper. His wings, coming through a slit in the back of his long, grubby white overall, appeared to belong to someone much taller, and their tips were dragging on the ground.

Clearly he wasn't a patient chap.

'Come on, I haven't all day. What's your number?'

I didn't intend to be harangued like this by a man with dentures and second-hand wings, a high-pitched voice and a Birmingham accent.

He'd rubbed me up the wrong way. I drew myself up to my full five feet seven and a half, and told him so. The extra half inch is important. Mike, my best mate, is just five seven and that bit extra is great for bragging rights when we're together. It helps in the pecking order.

'I don't know what you're talking about. I'm new here, I've just arrived and I don't have a number. Even if I had, why should I tell you? I don't know you from Adam. Anyway I have a splitting headache and would give anything for a nice cup of tea.' This last bit was me trying to soft-soap him. It didn't work.

He reacted with a deep sigh, like a man whose patience was running out after a long day, though why he should hold it against me personally I don't know. After all we had only just met, so I can't be held responsible for problems with his corns, piles or perhaps a nagging wife. He wasn't angry or aggressive – just a man life had not been kind to and who had become resigned to the fact.

'Anybody can see you're new here. But when you checked in at The Gate you were given a number and I need it. They tell new arrivals to write the number on the back of your hand until you can remember it. That's Standard Procedure.'

'Just look at your hand, and read it out to me, there's a good chap. How will I know if you're on my list or not if you won't tell me what your number is? The list is in number order – not by names.'

He was trying to patronise me and I didn't like it. Bite your tongue Martin, sort it out calmly, then find a nice caff somewhere for a sit-down and a mug of tea with a couple of aspirins.

I told him I hadn't come through any gate, and as far as I knew had simply materialised on that very spot just minutes before. I mentioned being beamed up by Scotty but my friend didn't seem to have much of a sense of humour. Or maybe he didn't watch much television. Well he was a Brummie, after all. The little man stared at me in disbelief.

'The only way in here is through The Gate. You can't come in otherwise, right? It isn't physically possible, take my word for it. Nothing ever works unless people follow the rules. Now tell me what I want to know. I'm a busy chap and people like you don't make it any easier.'

I began to feel sorry for him. He was just a bloke with a job to do. Then he upset me again.

'No.'

His voice was getting louder and his right eye was twitching.

'It won't work. I see now what your game is. You think you're being clever, don't you? Don't try the old soldier with me. I've been round long enough to see through your little trick. This is Holiday Section 32 and you want to come in but you're not entitled. You haven't qualified, have you? You're not on my list because you haven't qualified. You'll have to go back to your own Section, then come back when it's your turn. You're a queue jumper, that's what you are – a queue jumper – and I'm not going to fall for that old trick. You're a gatecrasher.'

He seemed to realise what he had said. Perhaps it was his first ever example of spontaneous wit. What a shame it clearly came out of the blue and was not of his making. Wherever it came from, he was claiming it as his. For a minute or two nothing could be heard but his squeaky voice repeating to himself the word *'Gatecrasher'*.

By now I'd had enough.

It didn't take the Brain of Britain to work out where I was, what with a man with wings and a reference to *'The Gates.'* With weddings, christenings, and a few funerals I knew some basic Theology – at least as much as your typical C of E man does these days. So up in Heaven I shouldn't have said some of the things I said, but this was becoming serious. I was fed up with being messed about and, anyway, I was feeling hungry and thirsty and my headache was as bad as ever.

So, after taking out some of my frustration on the guy I asked him where I could go to eat. Though I thought my point had been reasonably put, it still it seemed to upset him.

'Right. That's it. I've had enough. I'm trying to do my job and I've got a gatecrasher under my feet and getting in the way. Don't move from here while I sort you out.'

He took the bleeper from his pocket and tapped it vigorously with his fingers, muttering to himself as he did so – something about the batteries he was given to work with.

'Ah, there you are. That you 14? 273 Roberts here. Look, there's a man here who claims that he hasn't come in through Gates Department and he's got no docket.'

‘No, I know he can't have. But that's what he says and I can't budge him. I think he's just trying it on to get into the Holiday Annexe ahead of his turn.’

‘He’s a Gatecrasher.’

He chortled away to himself.

‘Get it? He’s a Gatecrasher. Good one isn’t it.’

‘Yes, it’s all mine. Just invented it. Completely original. You’re the first I’ve told it to.’

‘Of course he knows about the waiting list, otherwise why would he be trying it on like this?’

‘His name? No, he won't tell me. I'll try again.’

Suddenly his manner changed. His body stiffened as he drew himself to his full height. My earlier estimate of five feet and a little bit was less than fair - undoubtedly he was a full five feet four when he stood to attention.

‘Yes, Sir. Of course, Sir. At once, Sir.’

Roberts was oozing humility and smarm. It was most unedifying and reminded me of Uriah Heap on television a while back.

He turned to me.

‘Come on now. You've had your fun. We've all had a laugh.’

His face twisted into what he thought was a smile. The smile of a fellow conspirator in on the joke that just the two of them shared.

‘The joke’s over. Just tell me who you really are and your number. Then we can put you on the next shuttle back to your Section and you if you want you can go and get something to eat.’

The thing to do was to tell him what I knew, so I explained what I could. My name is – or was – Martin Douglas and that I have only just died. I think.

That I was driving north on the M6 when I was shunted into a bridge by some idiot driving a white Transit van with *'Palmers – Plumbers'* logo on its side. I surprised myself by remembering as clearly as I did but it's not every day you die, is it? Perhaps total recall is normal to the newly dead.

I remembered, but didn't tell him, that on Radio 2 Fred Astaire was singing *'Heaven, I'm in Heaven'* when it happened. Somehow I didn't think that he would have appreciated that.

He listened in silence, before responding.

'I'll tell you frankly, I don't believe a word of it. I'm due for my fourth gold watch in three years time, and this has never happened before in all my experience.'

'Now that I've listened, I'll make enquiries. Till I hear back you can go through that door into the Holiday Section. Go where you want. We know where to find you when we're ready for you. Don't try to Gatecrash out.'

Chortling away to himself he turned his back on me and went on his bleeper. Feeling like a naughty schoolboy being dismissed, I went through the door, pushing as I did against a creaking, stubborn turnstile that needed oiling, reminding me of my younger days supporting City.

***

During my discussions with Roberts the combination of my headache, hunger and his annoying presence had not given me time to look at my surroundings, but subconsciously I had noted that everything looked normal, that is as near as to what passes for normal round where I live.

Nothing at all to show where I was. No bright lights, no gold tipped fleecy-white clouds, No bands of Angels, no Heavenly Choirs. I didn't see anyone else – with or without a halo. Not what years of

Sunday School had led me to expect. Perhaps I've a case to make for a refund for all those pennies I'd put on the collection plates in my childhood. The wrong-size wings that Roberts had was the only sign of anything vaguely ethereal.

What Roberts had tried so hard to guard was a complete let-down. I found just an uninspiring view – merely an open flat area with patchy grass, basically a field and nothing else. At a distance I could see goal posts but no signs of a game. I looked again. There was a game of sorts going on in the distance that somehow I had missed. Perhaps it's that headache but how could I have not seen it moments before? Very strange.

A Holiday Annexe? It's all a big con. It's nothing more than a recreation ground – the sort you can find in most towns. Somebody was having me on.

As I watched the field changed. From an area of staggering dullness it changed to somewhere almost as unexciting, except that a few buildings had appeared. Somewhere I'd seen before but couldn't immediately place.

I'd seen *'Hi Di Hi'* on the telly and that was set in the fifties somewhere. It was something like that – an old-fashioned style holiday camp.

As I looked more closely I could see neat rows of separate wooden, single-storey buildings, each with its own gravel and grass surround carefully marked out with newly whitewashed stones. Waste bins everywhere and everything tidy – much too tidy for eyes used to contemporary Britain. No litter, no graffiti. Separate buildings at intervals that looked like toilet blocks or showers:– *'latrines'* was the word I was looking for that came into my head.

Strange though, among the figures I could see there were no women anywhere and everyone appeared to in blue. Air force blue.

Got it! Butlin's be blowed! I recognised where I was from memories of 40 or so years ago. R.A.F. Lytham St. Annes in the 'fifties.

'How the Hell did I get here of all places?'

Careful what you say Martin. That's probably the opposition you're talking about. They'll be the away team up here.

Something clicked. I'd been thinking how much Roberts reminded me of an N.C.O. I had run across at Lytham back in my two years spell of National Service.

I can't remember his name but he was the sort who would pull rank at the drop of a hat on anyone, but went all smooth and smarmy when anyone who outranked him was present. You know the sort. The sort they call a '*Jobsworth*' these days – a brownnoser. When I was in the mob he was the sort of bloke we used to say who would wear his sergeant's stripes on his pyjamas just to impress his wife.

Nearby on my left a young airman was being dressed down very publicly by someone I now remembered as Flight Sergeant Johnson (inevitably 'shorthouse' Johnson' to us erks). Words and phrases I thought I'd forgotten poured back from then – *'best-blue, 1250, U/T, 48 hour pass, last three (Douglas 372, Sir!)*.' My father, long gone now, always said that an ex-soldier never forgot his service number, and dad was one of those at the Somme in 1916. The fact that I was as far away from my national Service days as he had been from WWI when he said this to me put events into perspective.

The scene in front of me changed again. The huts vanished and I found myself standing near the ticket window of a busy railway station. A harassed looking man with a lot of baggage and several children was arguing with the clerk, and there was some dispute about fares for under-twelve's. The man behind the little window was not being very helpful. I couldn't see the face, but I'd seen that hair style somewhere recently.

The station was familiar, as was the clerk. He and I had clashed before when his fussy ways had upset me. It wasn't just me – he upset everyone.

Seeing a face I vaguely recognised I began to wonder. Would I see anyone here I knew well? Just then I saw my wife approaching. My ex-wife actually. The man she was with was my best friend. To be truthful he is virtually a stranger to me and I've only met him a couple of times, but he'd been my 'best friend' since he took my wife to make her my ex. I owe him a drink sometime. A large one.

I began to see an explanation for the weird things that were happening. Just try something else to check my theory, and then ? Q.E.D.

The scene changed again. Yes, there I was where I wanted to be. It was last Sunday. I was batting at one end, with Pete Scott at the other. The same bowler running up and delivering the same ball. Slow, inviting, tempting, and just wide of my off stick. This time, though, I was ready. I settled for a single as I hit the ball into the covers. Pete wasn't too pleased. At the end of the over he came down the wicket to talk to me.

'There was another run there, Martin. Getting old and slow then, are we? Cut back on the fags if that's what they're doing to you.'

I didn't bother arguing. He didn't know what I knew, did he? How was Pete to know he would have slipped and been run out if we had gone for the second? Anyway, it was the Annual Veterans Match and we were all being reminded how the days of taking quick singles were behind us. It was much easier to lean on the bat and gasp for breath than to take an extra run. Batting at the bowler's end was beginning to have considerable appeal.

Well: that confirmed my theory. Just think of where you want to be and there you are. Anywhere you like, when you like, and with anyone you choose. Great. And you could avoid people too, if you kept them out of your thoughts. And if you did remember them, well, all you had to do was think of something else.

I could even change history. Win the Ashes every series and thrash the Germans at penalty shoot-outs. Marvellous. No wonder there was a waiting list. Far and away the best holiday venue I knew or had ever heard of. You can keep your Blackpool, Southend or the Costa Blanca – me, I'd choose Holiday Centre 32 over any of them. Pity it looks as if you have to be dead to come here, though. There's a fortune to be made if someone can do something like it on earth. He'd make a real killing. Again, my choice of word made me think. Apt perhaps for here, but not for whatever direction England was from here.

Food. I was feeling ravenous by now. At Deaneworth Cricket Club they do a great ham salad so I'd decided to think myself back to the tea interval when my thoughts were interrupted by a voice from a loudspeaker.

'Calling Mr. Douglas. Mr. Martin Douglas.'

It wasn't 273 Roberts. Instead it was a deep, boomy voice with measured enunciation that sounded to me as somebody was part way through a course of elocution lessons.

'Would Mr. Douglas please leave by turnstile 44?'

He didn't sound like a man who was happy in his work. Probably looking up all his old clients from his day job as Director of a Funeral Parlour.

I saw Gate 44 and went through it to see Roberts with another man. This other chap was well over six feet tall, with ruddy cheeks, thin and erect with the look of an ex-military man who wants to be seen as ex-military. His toothbrush moustache, black suit and bowler hat told me at once that he was some sort of boss – even if a brief case instead of a clip-board didn’t give it away.

His umbrella surprised me. Somehow angel's wings, a bowler hat and rolled umbrella didn't go together. Rain in Heaven? Another question for my ever-lengthening list.

Roberts had an *‘I told you so’* look on his face. As the new man spoke Roberts began to nod his head at almost every word, clearly trying to impress his boss. To me he looked more like one of those nodding dogs you see in the backs of cars.

‘Mr. Douglas.’

It was the voice I had just heard on the loudspeaker.

…’Sir.’

After what I’d had to put up with earlier that caused my eyebrows to shoot up I can tell you.

He continued. ‘My name is Mr. Merry. I have recently been made Cognizant of the Exceptional – I might say almost Unique Circumstances concerning this matter of your presence here. The explanation which you gave my subordinate has been Invigilated – most thoroughly of course – and its Veracity has been Confirmed by Head Office.’

At the reference to Head Office his voice lowered and I half expected him to genuflect. He waved what looked like a fax at me. 'It puts Head Office into what I can only describe as a *'Dilemmable Situation'* at this moment in time.'

The more the man spoke with his repeated stressing of where he thought capital letters ought to be, the more obvious it was where Roberts had learned his speaking style.

'Quite simply, Mr. Douglas, you Should Not Be Here........Yet.'

As he said that one word, Mr Merry watched me to see if its significance had registered with me. It had, and it must have shown on my face.

'There is an Individual of the same Nomenclatural Adjunct as yourself who should have arrived up Here and hasn't, while you should still be Down There.' He made a gesture with his umbrella vaguely pointing downwards. So we do go up to Heaven then and people have been right all the time? We live and learn – or should it be die and learn?

'The problem is, Mr. Douglas, that you are Premature.'

'I want you to understand that what has happened is in no way due to any shortcomings in the Section which is under My Control. I am responsible for Fun and Entertainment in Section 327/H and this quite appalling lapse has been perpetrated Elsewhere. I am happy to report to you, Mr Douglas, that the person responsible for this gross error in the Records Department has been renovated to another post.'

Mr Merry looked across at his subordinate with relish. Roberts looked happier than at any time during our short acquaintance. Clearly they both knew the poor sod who was carrying the can for this clanger. It looked as if it had made their day.

‘We take no pleasure at another's downfall, but Standards Must Be Maintained.’

‘Head Office has impregnated me’ – he waved the paper again – ‘to arrange for your return Down There. All recollections of your time up Here will be impugned from your memory.’

He paused, apparently expecting me to speak. I took my cue.

‘Right,’ I said. ‘I understand. I’m here by mistake and these things do happen – even here, apparently’. I couldn’t resist getting that dig in at this pair of clowns. ‘But I don’t want to go yet – I’m going to eat, have a cup of tea and a couple of aspirins.’

‘Anyway, while I’m here there are people I want to talk to. The Captain of the *'Mary Celeste'* for starters. Then there's ....’

He held up his hand. I found myself unable to speak, no matter how hard I tried.

‘The matter has been decided by The Highest Authority. Your wishes are of no imperative. You are to Go Back.’

‘And no, Mr. Douglas. I am not permitted to revelate to you when Your Time will be.’

Roberts spoke next – for the first time since his superior had arrived.

‘You must leave at once. You can't stop here any longer.’

I felt myself going weaker by the second as the two figures in front of me began to disappear. One second they were there – then they’d gone. Only Roberts’ voice with its strong Birmingham accent remained.

His voice died away and my last thought was of the Cheshire cat and its grin. Then I remembered nothing else.

Back to the black, silent void again.

***

The M6 around Birmingham is just about the busiest stretch of motorway in Europe – or so I'd been told. That day the traffic was exceptional but even so I knew I was in good time for my appointment. Jane had known that I needed an earlier start than usual that morning and had made me coffee and toast to kick off the day. She's a treasure that girl. I think it's getting near the time I popped the question and we really sorted ourselves out on a truly permanent basis.

I'd seen my exit sign and was easing down to leave the middle lane when the accident happened. A red Sierra similar to mine and directly behind me was hit by a Ford Transit van as we passed under a bridge. It looked bad, but by the time I could have done anything I was too far ahead. In my rear view mirror I could see lights flashing and the traffic behind was either stopped or stopping.

'Poor devils.' I thought. 'Somebody's number's up. Close – it almost could have been me.' Fred Astaire's song on my car radio at the time was one of those unfortunate coincidences that happen. Inevitable sometimes, I suppose.

***

I hardly know Birmingham at all. I'd been given brief directions by the buyer I was going to see at Atlas Engineering, but somehow I managed to get myself completely lost and was driving around in circles. To make it worse I had a splitting headache that I hadn't been aware of until the accident. The crash must have upset me, I suppose. As well as that I felt exceptionally hungry. Very strange. It wasn't all that long since I'd had a stop and a snack at Watford Gap. There was also a niggling feeling that there was something I couldn't remember but wanted to.

'Found it.'

In relief I pulled off the road, driving under an archway and failing to see the sign over the gate.

I was rummaging in my brief case for my notes when there was a vigorous tapping at my window. I wound it down to see a little man, who couldn't have been much over five feet in height, wearing a grubby white overall and with a top pocket full of coloured pens. He was nearly bald and what hair he had was combed up and across from below his left ear.

The man was shouting and pointing at something. He had a very strong Birmingham accent.

'You must leave at once. You can't stop here any longer.'

I saw the notice I'd missed as I drove in. There it was.

'PRIVATE. NO ENTRY.

ADMISSION BY APPOINTMENT ONLY.'

The little man was becoming quite agitated.

'You can't stop here', he repeated. 'Please leave at once.'

He pointed to the way out, thrusting a card into my hand as he did so. He turned away before I had time to ask him for directions, and as he did I saw that there was a rip in the back of his overall. As if I hadn't enough to do right now without noticing things like that. Unpleasant little man.

To add to my problems my brand new watch had stopped. Well, as they say, it would be right twice a day – as long as it's 9.58.13. God, I need a cuppa and a couple of aspirins, this headache's getting worse.

Eventually I reached my destination and we did enough business to make it worthwhile. And there was a promise, or at least a hint, of repeat business in due course. With part of my income from commission that's always good to hear. About the only thing so far today that had been half-way decent. As I headed back south my head was still throbbing, so more tea and aspirins were needed and even a grotty motorway meal would do for now as I felt so hungry.

As I was looking for a parking spot the car radio switched automatically to one of its regular updates on road conditions, so I waited a moment and heard a woman's voice telling me I was dead. Or at least my namesake was after an accident earlier on the M6 northbound.

The car's driver had been killed. He had been identified as Martin Douglas, aged 58. Next of Kin had been informed. Two other men, both plumbers from Warrington, were in hospital. The Police wanted witnesses. The road was now clear.

Obviously it was the crash I'd just avoided that morning.

I shuddered. Talk about someone walking over your grave. I know now what that means. Same age as me, too. Those coincidences stunned me. I tried to calculate the chances of accidents involving similar cars, even down to the same colour, with a driver the same name and age, but my maths just weren't up to it.

The news shook me up very badly. I picked up a tray and went along the counter, choosing something with chips. Quite honestly, I couldn't have told you what was on my plate, for despite being as hungry as I was, my mind was on the crash earlier. Some blokes turn to a bottle of the hard stuff when they need solace, I like tea and drink gallons of the stuff. So with a cuppa I settled at my table.

First things first. I reached into my top pocket for the pack of aspirin tablets I always carry with me. With the tablets my fingers pulled out the card that man in Birmingham had given me. I used to work for a printing firm so I could recognize it as a cheap, mass-produced card any back-street jobbing printer would knock out for you. It was grey with shiny black embossed printing inside a black border. Its message was clear enough.

J. P. Merry and Associate. Funeral Directors.

Interments with Dignity and Respect.

Caskets put away for small deposit.

See us before you go. Don't leave it too late.

The reminder on the card made me feel guilty. I hadn't phoned Jane. The poor girl will be worried sick if she's heard the news. I rushed my chips and something and went off to find a callbox.

What is round the corner for us? Nobody really knows and personally I wouldn't want to. An early death maybe? Who knows? Perhaps the little chap in the white overall is trying to tell me something about my mortality. He might even have contacts up there – a sort of private early warning system. That would be useful in his line of business.

What a bloody awful day. The crash on the M6 that I missed by just seconds, getting lost in Brum, that silly little man getting under my skin, a splitting headache that won't go, something that feels important that I can't remember and then hearing about my namesake being killed. Gloomy thoughts about the future. The Grim Reaper waiting to harvest up more of us from down here? It couldn't go any worse, surely. I'm a fittish fifty-eight year old, after all. What am I worrying about?

***

Extract from the report by the Coroner, Dr. R. T. Michaelson, at the inquest of Martin William Douglas.

'There were several witnesses and ample evidence was collected. The witnesses were queuing for a phone box to become available so were watching the users of the telephones closely.

The deceased was seen making a telephone call, then he appeared to drop something and bend down to pick it up, probably the 50 pence coin that the police found inside the booth. He was seen to bang his head on the glass wall of the telephone booth and fall to the ground. Very quickly people went to help but found Mr. Douglas was dead. Several of the witnesses referred to their surprise that such an apparently minor blow caused Mr. Douglas' death.

Evidence from Home Office Pathologist Professor Andrew Sowerby showed puzzling anomalies. Professor Sowerby referred to the post mortem examination. The deceased, at 58, was in reasonable condition for a man of his age and there were no physical reasons, other than a head injury, to cause his death.

Examination of the skull showed that its thickness was normal and on that basis a slight blow to the head should not have killed him.

However, Professor Sowerby's examination did reveal that the skull was – in his words – like a 'glued together eggshell, or a completed three-dimensional jigsaw puzzle.' He found that the head had been very badly damaged but appeared to have healed or been restored in some way that he could not understand. In his view the severe damage to the head had been very recent, as had the restoration work. What he found was unlike anything in his experience, and he could find no comparable case in the specialist literature and the files available from any recognised source worldwide. The restoration work could conceivably been done on a skull, but he found it impossible to see how it could have been performed on a living person at the present level of medical and scientific knowledge and skill.

The deceased's Medical Files did not show any injuries to the head. The condition of the skull after what had happened meant that the slightest damage, any sort of minor blow to the head, could have caused death instantaneously.

The Coroner passed on his sympathies to Miss Jane Pargeter, the partner of the deceased, and to his other relatives and friends.

Coroner's verdict. Misadventure.'

ON THE PASSING OF AN IMPORTANT MAN.

(Published in *Winamop*. January 2013).

Such a sad day.'

'A great man.'

'He will be sorely missed.'

'The entire country will mourn his passing.'

'All the good he did in his lifetime.'

'What dignity his widow is showing.'

'And four young children too.'

'Oh, those poor children.'

'I see a man from the press is over there writing names down.'

'And HRH is coming too.'

'Are those television cameras over there?'

'I wonder if those cameras are from the BBC or one of the others.'

'Don't those Cardinal's robes look magnificent?'

'I hear his name is likely to come up for a posthumous honour.'

'Look at those angelic children from the Home.'

'The Home bears his name, you know.'

'One of those children is holding a wreath.'

'What a lovely gesture.'

'Aren't those children sweet?'

'Those little boys are from his Foundation.'

'I really must have a word with the man from the *Times*.'

'The P.M's car has arrived, I understand.'

'It is so important that one's name is spelled correctly.'

'Does his Children's Charity publish full accounts, one wonders?'

'All so sudden – in bed, they say.'

'Apparently he wasn't at home when it happened.'

'The cameraman is photographing the American Ambassador.'

'Ought we to move over to that side?'

'The Cardinal has joined the Prime Minister for a photograph of the two of them together.'

'I think we might see better from over the other side, my dear.'

'One does hear stories, but is today the time to air them?'

'You appreciate that what I am saying is in the strictest confidence.'

'Eighty thousand, you say?'

'I heard there's a property involved too.'

'It really must go no further.'

'Of course, his origins were always a little, shall I say – unclear?'

'There are hints – I will say no more – about his background.'

'We were just saying, Sir John, what good works he did. But have you heard……?'

'Will she be here, do you think?'

'Surely she won't come here on this day of all days?

'Much younger than his widow, of course.'

'I did hear that there are rumblings in the City.'

'Two hundred and fifty thousand has been mentioned.'

'They were in bed together when it happened, you know.'

'I heard half a million.'

'His Paris apartment is quite remarkable.'

'That's as well as the one in Rome.'

'Do you think the papers know?'

'Oh, they will.'

‘Very soon I expect.’

‘I understand the press will pay well for information – especially about a scandal.’

‘Shall we circulate and hear what people are saying?’

‘Is that her do you think?’

‘Surely not.’

‘Not today.’

‘I suppose it would be a tabloid that would pay most for information.’

‘It might be her.’

‘She looks the sort.’

‘Would it be the News Editor who would handle that sort of thing?’

‘And isn’t that his brother with her too?’

‘Isn’t he like the deceased?’

‘It is her, I’m sure of it.’

‘It’s easy to see what attracted him, isn’t it?’

‘George! That’s enough of that!’

‘She and the widow are heading the same way.’

‘They’re going to bump into each other.’

‘Do try to get closer to them both.’

‘Pardon me, may we pass?’

‘Is that better?’

‘Can you see them together?’

‘Can you hear better now?’

‘Is your name on the list the press man is compiling?’

‘No, I can’t catch what they’re saying.’

‘One’s name has to in *The Times* list, of course.’

‘I’ve made sure they’ve spelled it correctly.’

‘Such a sad day.’

THE ONE THAT GOT AWAY.

(Published in *First Edition*. March 2010)

I'm not a fisherman. The last time I fished for anything I was about nine and used a jam jar to catch tiddlers. It didn't work. I didn't catch a thing but I do remember that my wellies leaked, my socks were wet through, and my mother wasn't pleased when I got home. Anyway, I diverge. What I was beginning to say was that like everyone else, I know that fishermen are reputed to have great stories about *'the one that got away.'* They all can come up with a tale about this massive fish that was uncatchable, and how close they were to doing the impossible when the line snapped or something.

Now Fred Graham I know for a fact wasn't a fisherman. Fishing to Fred was sport, and he wanted it banned like bull-fighting and game-bird shooting. And you should have heard him on the subject of fox-hunting – that really got him going. But Fred had his own tale of what might have been; one that matched any that a chap in waders and a hat with things pinned into it could tell.

His story went back about twenty years to when he was a young, ambitious antiques dealer in his first shop. Through a contact – actually his brother-in-law, a chap who knew a local solicitor well, and more importantly had enough hold on him to know where the bodies were buried – Fred had managed to get a very generous lease on premises spacious enough to allow him to deal in furniture. He had a few pieces of porcelain and pottery around the shop, and a couple of prints on the walls for show, but furniture was definitely Fred's thing.

He'd been in his shop about eighteen months by this time, and it wasn't going well. He'd managed, with difficulty, to pay the current year's rent, and was already beginning to worry about the one that was due in September. As well as strings being pulled to give him extra space, the rent was lower than it should have been, but even so, Fred knew he had to do something or go under. He had a 'Board Meeting' – he always called it that when he needed to do something – even though he had no wife to tell him what to do, or partner to discuss things with, and the meeting was inside his head. The big decision he came to was to change his advertising and marketing strategy and to go upmarket.

Instead of posting adverts in the papers and aiming at the local people, as anything to sell, was hardly likely to make him a staggering profit – Fred was to 'go to the toffs. They always have plenty of it.' As he put it – 'The folks round here are decent enough people, but they haven't got two ha'pence to rub together. I'll never get stuff from them that will get me into the London Salerooms. *'London Salerooms'* – that was Fred's El Dorado, his ambition and dream, and he could bore for Britain on the subject. His master plan didn't involve changing completely: the cheap ads in the local free papers weren't to be dropped, but he was going to splash out on a couple of adverts in *Country Life* and the glossy, lavishly presented *County Times* that came out monthly. He was fond of quoting the cliché 'speculate to accumulate.' He nearly changed his mind when he rang up to check on what it was going to cost him to put a quarter page ad in them, but after radically cutting back on the space he was buying, he booked for the next three issues. He approved the proofs for both, then when he held the full printed June issues in his hands, all of his instinctive *'up the workers'* feeling came to the surface.

'Fancy weddings, big hats, young women with big arses in jodhpurs who look like their nags, double-barrelled names – they're all there. Plus country houses like hotels. It shouldn't be allowed. People like that won't deal with the likes of me. They'll be on the jolly old blower to Cousin Sebastian down at Christie's or Bonham's I expect. Fred Graham won't get a sniff. I've made a big mistake.' Fred was a lovely man, a real pussy cat when you got to know him, but he had this *'To the barricades'*, and *'Wait till the revolution comes, comrades'* attitude. Over a pint or three he would admit he didn't really believe in it, all he wanted was a reasonable living and an early retirement to Spain. That all came from a week in Benidorm three years earlier he'd obviously enjoyed.

And it began to look more and more as if he had miscalculated. 'Nary a nibble' as Fred put it. In the middle of the third month, the final month in his new campaign, Fred was beginning to despair. He could just about raise the money for the next year's lease but he wasn't sure he wanted to commit himself. There were other options. A picture dealer he knew offered to let him share space in his shop, but on a rent plus commission on sales basis. That didn't suit Fred. He could go to a cheaper shop, but that would have meant less space, so reducing his stock, and he had no wish to become known as *'Fred – that bloke who used to deal in furniture.'* Rented space in an Antiques Centre in the main shopping area might be a consideration, but to Fred, it would be almost like working for someone else. Or he could start dealing at Antiques Fairs. That was what Fred decided to do, and he would arrange the end of the lease in two weeks time. The ultimate option – finding 'a proper job' – was never seriously considered. Fred knew that was the end of the line and he didn't feel he'd sunk that far – not yet anyway.

In one of his final weeks before cutting his losses and leaving, Fred was trying to sell a fifties G Plan bureau to a young couple. Clearly they liked it – something that made Fred wonder if tastes were changing, and somewhere along the line he'd missed the beginnings of a trend. Certainly he was regularly being offered pieces from that era, the sort of stuff he'd grown up with at home with his parents – but selling it was a different matter. He had plenty of it, too much in fact, and finally he cut the price to the bone to make a sale. It was his first for two days. They discussed delivery – the young man had a *'friend with a van'* and that would save him paying Fred to take it round to their house. That suited Fred; they shook hands and cash was exchanged for a written receipt. As they left, it was a relieved Fred who noticed, for the first time, an elderly lady hovering near the back of the room. *'Hovering*' was the word that Fred used and he said it was the right one. Uncertain and clearly in strange territory – that's what he said.

This 'old girl,' as he first described her, was obviously uneasy. A complete stranger to him, dressed in drab and dreary old-fashioned clothes he remembered, Fred went to her and learned that she wanted someone to go out to her house, look at some things and give her a price for buying. She said her name was Thorne, and had an address on a piece of paper; Fred glanced at it, knew approximately where it was, and agreed to go next day. More interested in selling than buying at present, he knew very well that he had to buy to stay in business. She was very vague about what he would see when he got there; beyond saying there was some old furniture of good quality. He heard that from nine out of ten of his callers – they all had something *'like what they'd seen on that telly programme last weekend when they said it was worth fifteen thousand'* so he took little notice, but agreed to go the next day.

He arrived on time and his first reaction was that the old girl had one of the apartments that he assumed the place had been converted to. Charborough Manor it was called and though architecture was not Fred's thing he could see the house was old. He guessed at Elizabethan but wouldn't have bet money on it. He drove up to the main door and pulled the chain he found half-way up the wall. Rusty and needing some oil it worked to the extent of bringing a young woman in maid's uniform to the door.

On giving his name and asking for Miss Thorne, he was ushered into a side room, told that Lady Millicent would see him shortly and asked to wait. Within minutes the old lady appeared and asked him to follow. 'There are several rooms to look in and something in each for you to see, Mr. Graham.' As part of his new strategy, Fred had taken to carrying a notebook with him, so, looking very businesslike and efficient, with the book, pencil and digital camera in his hands with a wind-up metal tape in his pocket, he followed the old lady. He soon established that small talk was not her way and instead he concentrated on what he was doing. After all, it was a thirty mile round trip in a petrol-guzzling elderly Volvo estate, so if nothing else, he had expenses to cover.

Now, what I know about furniture – antique or modern – you could write on the back of a penny black, so for this, you and me, we're both taking Fred's word for it. But what Fred told me later was that it was like a child's fairyland – a magic grotto. He threw a few names at me – Chippendale and Robert Adam I do remember because I had heard of them; as well as some continental sounding people – but he said it was like a dream come though. He said for a few minutes it was like being on a tour of somewhere like Buckingham Palace or Blenheim or somewhere, with the public being barred, and you having the time to look around properly and examine things. He followed the old lady – by then he'd started to address her with a lot more respect than when he first arrived and his views on social status and class distinction were under wraps with the smell of money about – and listed whatever she pointed at. Only certain items were to go on his list, but a blind man making a selection could hardly have gone wrong in such a situation the quality was so high.

Fred clarified the position with Miss Thorne / Lady Millicent that – 'Yes, she did want him to make an offer on any items she pointed to – but, and it was a very big 'but,' Fred was the first to view but others were to be asked later to quote'. This was all news to Fred. There was little worse for a dealer than to be told that he was the first of several, and his offer was to be the starting point – the benchmark – for all who followed. He felt like leaving there and then, but common sense prevailed. He did his best to explain how unfair the situation was, and said that it was normal for the first bidder to be given a chance to respond with a re-bid later. He made the point as forcibly as he could without antagonising the old lady, but didn't think he was getting anywhere. The point about the final bidder being in the best position didn't seem to register with her or was simply beyond her understanding.

This unwanted news slowed down his reaction to something obvious he should have noticed earlier. For all the quality he was being offered, nothing was as it should be. There were several massive dining tables, but at each were just two, possibly three chairs instead of the expected six or more. And the important head of table chair – the carver, the one with arms – had gone from each. Assuming they were elsewhere in other rooms, or being stored somewhere, he asked, in the excessively polite, smarmy way he had taken on since the smell of money became so strong, (Fred's own description to me of his demeanour by now) where they were and could he please see them while he was here – 'just to confirm they matched, nothing more.' He also had noticed, even though pottery and porcelain was not his field, some magnificent pieces – like a magnificent Sevres vase where ideally a pair should have been.

'Where they are now, Mr. Graham, I have no idea. You'd have to ask Mr. Tremayne that. He will know.'

'Tremayne? – oh, he's our family solicitor.'

'When I first wished to dispose of some of the furniture – there's no-one else after me in the family, y'know, I'm the last of the Charborough's and Death Duties will be a terrible charge on the estate, I called him in. He suggested that rather than sell off complete sets of anything I should sell something from each; so leaving enough to remember how they had been. And that was the pattern we followed. Every time I needed to sell something, just a few odd chairs or a vase and things went. A sensible way of doing things, don't you think?'

Still hoping, though less and less as the minutes passed, Fred made a noise that he hoped would sound polite and non-committal to Lady Millicent. Already resigned to losing out to someone else, his thoughts about solicitors were unrepeatable. Before today his personal rating would have put them alongside politicians at about 3 on a scale of 1 to 10. After what he had just heard they would be even lower. Afterwards Fred did tell me some facts and figures as a for-instance, but don't ask me to remember them. All I do remember is that what this Tremayne man had done had massively lowered the value of the furniture by splitting it up like that. To me later, he referred to Tremayne as 'an imbecile, philistine, cretin' and some other less polite terms.

For form's sake, and to try to salvage his own pride, Fred tried again but he knew he'd lost. Her mind was made up. Three dealers, three visits, three offers to consider – a word with Mr. Tremayne and there you are – matter sorted and she wouldn't be bothered again. Not for a while, anyway till she needed to sell again. And with his knowledge of solicitors' doings from the inside he imagined that this Tremayne bloke would have *'his little earner'* in the deal somewhere – and not with Fred Graham, either.

Fred left for home a sad man. Naturally he had left bids on everything, but he knew he was wasting his time and nothing would ever come of this tantalising glimpse of real money. Even with what remained of the butchered sets he could have made a substantial amount and, during it, made a start on realising his dream. As it was, the shop would go and he would be getting up very early nearly every day, loading and unloading his van, to go off to God knows where to a tatty little fair to earn a crust. At least he didn't have a wife and kids to worry about – it was going to be hard enough to support himself. I later found out from Fred that for a while he became suicidal and only some inner strength stopped him before it was too late.

All of that was some time ago. We don't see each other much now since I moved away, but the last time we did have a drink together, a dejected and worn-out Fred had visibly aged far more than he should have. He did marry and has a couple of kids, but that went sour and he doesn't see either of them much. And he's not in the furniture business these days. Well, not what he would call the furniture trade. Fred now works in a trading estate at Winford where they make flat-pack tables and chairs. His job is something to do with the glue that he says is about 90% of what they call wood. If you do run into him, I shouldn't pursue that line of discussion at all. And don't, please; don't ever get onto the subject of fisherman's tales with him. He'll have one to tell you that will top any one of yours.

‘WELL, YOUR HONOUR, IT’S LIKE THIS.’

(Published in *Delinquent*. December 2012).

Next week I have to go and see this woman who has a whole string of letters after her name to convince her I’m not barmy. Then she’s got to see the magistrate before I go back to court. And like so much else that’s bad in my life, it’s all down to my ex. Let me explain.

When Freda went off with her fancy man, that bloke from the Co-op Funeral service, we sorted out a divorce. I kept the house – with the mortgage – she took most of our savings. End of story I thought. Starting off with a clean sheet. Apart from not having much money I was content with that and glad to see the back of her. She also took the Nissan and our dogs, two toy poodles, Victoria and Albert – Vicky and Bertie. Bertie was a nice little chap, but Vicky was a real handful. Wilful, bossy, but certainly trainable – at dog training classes she showed she could be when she wanted to be – but the moment she was outside again she went back to being her normal difficult self. Frankly I was glad to get rid of her almost as much as I was of the wife, and anyway, I’ve always really been a cat person.

Then, after I’d had a lovely, peaceful relaxed month of being single, one evening there was a knock at the door. It was Freda. ‘This so and so dog, I’ve had enough of her. We always said she looked like your mother so you can have her.’ With that she plonked Vicky into my arms and flounced off. I haven’t seen her since.

Vicky went wild – licking, barking, jumping up at me, running round the house, then she settled down and went to sleep. I wasn’t happy about it all, but that was probably part of Freda’s intention. I suppose I’d better explain this thing about looking like my mother.

Actually it is true. Back in happier times we'd both said the same thing – that when you saw Vicky from certain angles she looked like my mother – who's been dead now for years. A longish, oval face and large sad, brown eyes.

So, I was stuck with a dog I didn't like and didn't want, a dog that I could see giving me problems – what with what to do with her when I was out at work all day, and as for any hopes I had for a renewal of a sex-life – well, let's just say she wouldn't help. My short-lived freedom went downhill from there.

Home from work next day I was dozing in front of the fire when this voice woke me up. 'Why don't you talk to me? Tell me about your job and what you've been up to. Don't forget I've been on my own all day with no-one to talk to.' In a bit of a stupor I tried to bring myself back to being fully awake, wondering about my dream. I knew the voice, even though I hadn't heard it for about fifteen years or so. I opened my eyes and there was the dog, staring at me. 'Come on, you're awake now, Kevin. Let's have a chat.'

I thought I'd lost the plot – that I was bonkers, I really did. I wasn't though, as I was to find out. Those few words opened a floodgate. Vicky / mother / whoever / whatever – from that second evening back has talked, and talked, and talked. Incessantly. To me, at me, over me, through me, whatever whichway. She never stops. Nag, nag, nag. I never could stand it when she was alive and I can't now. No wonder Dad left her all those years since. The thing is, she only talks to me when there are just the two of us. If there are other people about, when I'm taking her for a walk for instance, she's just a small, white poodle. So how do I tell this woman when I see her next week what the truth really is? She'll never believe me. There's no way I can prove it.

So, this went on for a couple of months and I couldn't see any end to it. I suppose I could have taken her out miles away and abandoned her, but I wouldn't do that to any animal, certainly not to my mother. And as for trying to find a home for her, I reckon she would straight away have chosen to start to talk to anyone she went to, and she'd have the police or the RSPCA or somebody round here in a flash with a complaint about cruelty or something.

Then one day I fancied a run to the seaside. It was early April, warm and pleasant and I live just a few miles inland from the coast. So I put mother's lead on and we went to West Bay and parked up. I had an ice-cream from the little kiosk – they do that lovely soft stuff that comes out of a machine in swirls – and then we set off for a walk along the front. Coming towards us was an old chap in a wheelchair, being pushed by a young woman who looked as if she was from the social services – a carer they call them, I believe. It turned out that that's what she was.

As we got closer, mother became very agitated and as excited as I've ever seen her. She tried to pull me towards the wheelchair, and as we drew level she jumped up at the old man, and bit him two or three times in the thigh and hand. Obviously it was all a bit frantic with the woman trying to take the man out of range and me pulling mother off him. She – the woman – was shouting at me and trying to make a phone call on her mobile at the same time. The fine day had brought people out and a small crowd gathered. In response to her call a Social Services mini-bus drove up, and they bundled the old chap into it and drove away. She stayed and told the story to a policeman who had arrived by then. He took all the details and said I'd be hearing more about it.

Inevitably mother had an explanation. To her it was a simple enough matter. The old chap, she said, was my father and she wanted to pay him back for all the 'misery, grief and aggravation' (her words) that he'd given her years before. Nothing would shift her and she just could not see that she'd done anything wrong. I must admit, when I think back now I can see it was him. Obviously older but certainly my dad. I'd long assumed he'd died years before.

The outcome was that I was up in court on a charge of allowing an animal to be a danger to the public. I'd not taken any advice from anyone and decided the best thing was to tell the whole story to the magistrate exactly as it happened. That's why I'm to see a Psychiatrist next week.

My problems haven't finished there either. I had a sister – much older than I am. We never got on. In fact I actively disliked her and felt that trouble was never far away when she was around. Mother tells me that she, my sister Vera, is now a border-collie down at the Rescue Kennels over at Poole. How she'd heard about it I don't know, but she wants me to go over there and adopt Vera and give her a home with us. I don't see how I can get out of it. And there goes my wanting a cat. Vera hated them.

There's only one good thing about it that I can see about it. When I tell the beak that I've got an elderly mother to support and keep a home for her, it might be enough to keep me out of gaol. Just a thought. I think that's what I'll tell him when I do go back there on the 28th.

DOUBLE WHAMMY.

(Published in *Winamop*. January 2015)

I gave up smoking and had my first vasectomy years ago – both in the same week. To be honest it's ancient history now so I'd pretty well forgotten that the two events happened as close to each other as they did. Till the other night, that is, down at the *White Hart* when we were talking about anniversaries. It gave me a chance to pitch in for bragging rights for the evening when I told the lads about it. I reckon I won hands down.

Yes, I did say *'first vasectomy'*. It was quite simple really. I'd had to go back and have the snip done for a second time after the routine retest had found my system wasn't clear – apparently my tubes joined up by themselves and they shouldn't have. Naturally enough I put it down to simply being more virile than ordinary men – something the blokes down in the pub didn't see quite the way I did. The doc actually said at the time that I'm now on record somewhere in *Lancet* or one of the medical journals as I'm so special. That's worth having on your CV, isn't it? And I haven't touched a cigarette since then either – now that is something I'm really proud of. Quite a boast from a man who'd been on sixty a day up to then. Pete Marks bought me a pint on the strength of my 'double whammy' as he called it. He's been trying to give up as long as I've known him. He still went through nearly a pack in that one evening.

Jimmy Parsons had started us off by saying it was exactly a year since his brother Rob died, and the discussion and recollections followed on from there. I'd known Rob for years and the rest of the gang knew him just as well as I did. The two of them, offspring of a middle-aged marriage, were physically similar – see them together and you'd know they were from the same pod – but temperamentally they were as different as chalk and cheese. Jimmy, the younger by about two years, is quick, bright and great company. Rob – well he was Rob. Never the sharpest knife in the drawer he didn't socialise a lot and when he did, it showed. He wasn't backward or anything, nothing like that, but he was just sulky, self-centred and when he wasn't being grouchy he was dull, boring and someone to be avoided when you saw him coming.

'Limited' is perhaps the best word to describe him. No conversation, he didn't even have a special peculiar obsession that went with his temperament – something to baffle and bore us silly with, like collecting penny blacks or trying to solve the identity of Jack the Ripper. If he did turn up for a drink he'd just fill up space in the corner for a couple of hours, get his round in on time, and that was that. So you'll gather he wasn't missed too much when he fell off his perch. It's always sad when someone you know dies in his forties like he did, so we paid our respects, sent a wreath from the group of us at our local and Jos Smithers went to the crematorium with Jimmy and his family to represent us all: then we more or less forgot about brother Rob.

The discussion fizzled out as there was a feeling we were all getting a bit morbid about deaths and funerals and things so the topic became next week's international at Wembley. Somehow the way England have been playing lately that seemed almost as depressing.

During the talk about football it was clear that Jimmy P was in a bit of a world of his own. I put it down to the fact that he was probably thinking about Rob and obviously the others thought the same, so we all had a go at trying to chivvy him along to snap out of it. He did eventually brighten up a bit and started talking about his brother and a secret; a secret he'd been asked to keep for over thirty years. He'd respected the shared confidence all that time. Somehow Jimmy felt that if the secret was to be disclosed at some stage, when could be better than now when he was with his special pals who had all known his brother and his strange ways? The story Jimmy told us went something like this.

***

'When Rob and I were lads – I was about twelve and Rob that couple of years older, so we're talking well over thirty years back – Mum and Dad took us up to Blackpool to see the Illuminations. It was a coach thing on a Saturday from Shadwell's Tours down on Bridge Street in town. You've all probably done the same sort of trip – the coach gets there late morning, everybody has a few hours on their own in Blackpool, then when it's dark the 'bus goes up and down the front, you make all the right noises about the lights, then you go home and get back in the early hours. You know the sort of thing.'

There were nods all round as the memories poured back – some of us now as parents with our own kids taking them off to see the Lights: as well as when we were children ourselves and remembering the excitement and the silver coin for the first kid to spot the Tower in the distance.

'Rob and I were at that age when we didn't want to be seen with our folks all the time and felt we could manage on our own. Just like now – go to the seaside anytime and you'll see kids like we were then – embarrassed-looking, tagging along several paces behind, trying hard to look as if they're grown up and not with mum and dad. At that awkward in-between age – too old to be with their parents and too young to be let off the leash. So, the Parsons family, parents and boys, struck a deal.

We lads were given some money and a place and time to meet up again for getting on to the coach for the drive along the prom and going home. We were told very clearly we had to be there ready on time; and that meant both of us – definitely no splitting up.'

'The moment Rob and I were on our own, we began to argue about what to do. I wanted to go to the top of the Tower and Rob didn't. He had nowhere especially he wanted to go or anything to see, but he simply didn't want to do what I wanted. No reason why he should, of course, but at least my plan was something definite and not just aimless wandering. I thought he was just being cussed, and we all know how cussed he could be when he wanted to be – in spades. It was almost inevitable we would split up. Rob was my elder brother and so supposed to be the one with more sense, but even by then I'd realised that the extra couple of year's difference hadn't made him brighter – just older, that's all. I felt I knew better even as a kid, so Rob started to sulk and hid round a corner and I couldn't find him. I reckoned I spent half an hour or so just looking for him before I gave up. There was nothing for it other than to go off, spend my pocket money, enjoy myself and hope Rob turned up on time. Of course, Rob being Rob – he didn't.'

'When I got back to the big coach park near the Pleasure Beach – and I made sure I was early just in case – our parents were already there. I tried to explain what had happened and all Hell broke loose. Obviously they wouldn't have a clue where to start looking for their missing boy so they had no choice but to wait. The coach driver held on for about ten minutes longer than he should have and that was all he could do. The rest of the folks in the coach were getting very impatient and so he had to go leaving behind three upset and angry people. Rob turned up about five minutes after the ‘bus had gone and inevitably he was in serious trouble.’

‘For some reason peculiar only to Rob, he didn’t seem too bothered. He never did really explain properly what he’d been up to but just made a gruff apology and some vague excuse about confusing the time we’d all arranged to meet. Then he seemed to retreat inside his own head and simply just took all the grumbling and telling-off without showing as much reaction as I’d expected. So we didn’t see the lights that year except what we could manage to see by walking up and down the prom for a while. The driver collected us all on his way back and a very tired and subdued Parsons family finally got home in the early hours of Sunday morning.’

‘At first Rob wouldn’t tell me any more than he told Mum and Dad. Then, about a week later, when he was still very much in the doghouse at home, he took me on one side and told me something of where he’d been and what he’d done in Blackpool. Nothing like the nonsense about mixing up the time that he’d invented. What Rob told me was weird – about being on the Golden Mile, ambling along and seeing an advertising sign that intrigued him. In fact he’d written the words down so he could tell me exactly what it said. He even included a spelling mistake that he had underlined when he saw it. Spelling was one thing Rob was good at.’

‘Learn what the future holds. See the world renowned clairvoyant Gipsy Leona Felixa and she will tell you all. As consulted by Eminent People and <u>Goverments</u> the world over.’

‘Rob, being Rob, went in to the little booth, paid his two bob or whatever it was back then, was offered a choice of having his palm read or, as an alternative, this woman would look into her crystal ball and see what it foretold. She personally felt that this was better for the sitter – and well worth the extra it would cost.’ Jimmy shrugged as he told us. ‘We can guess which one Rob picked, can’t we?’

‘According to Rob he came out knowing that he was going to die when he was forty-five. His death would have something to do with water and flashing lights according to Gipsy Leona.’

‘To be honest I wasn’t sure if it wasn’t all a great big wind-up, but Rob seemed so sincere and deadly serious that I believed him. Anyway, when did anyone remember Rob trying to kid someone along for a practical joke? It just wasn’t his style’.

‘After he’d told me, Rob said that he didn’t want to discuss the matter again – ever. And he asked what he called ‘the biggest favour he could ask’ of me. He wouldn’t mention it again and I was never to tell anyone about it. I’d already told Rob that he was talking a load of nonsense and it was just a big catch-penny and he was a sucker to fall for it. But he stuck to his guns and so I agreed that it would stay a secret between us.’

By this time I was wrapped up in the story and I could see the others in our little ‘Gang of Five’ as we called ourselves were too. We threw in a few leading questions but Jimmy just told us to hear him out: there was more to come. He took a long drink from his pint, a drink he looked as if he needed, then resumed his tale.

‘You may find it hard to believe but the fortune-telling business wasn’t mentioned by either of us by as much as a single word ever again until about two years back. That’s well over thirty years of silence

– and that was all from Rob's choice. I know you'll probably find that strange but it's perfectly true. For me it had always been a load of old codswallop and though I had more or less forgotten about it, Rob obviously hadn't.'

'One Sunday morning Rob called round at the house. Maggie had gone round to her sister's, the boys were out at a football match somewhere and I was alone in the house. I reckon that Rob might have known all that before he came. Rob was like a man high on something. He didn't do drugs as far as I ever knew and he certainly wasn't drunk. What was the matter with him soon became clear.'

'Hey, bro. I've won. I've beaten the gipsy's curse. I'll live for years longer. Let's go and have a pint or three to celebrate.'

The story Rob told me was so weird I found it hard to believe. He said he'd been up to Blackpool the previous day. And it wasn't an impulse thing either. He said he'd driven there specifically to look for the Gipsy woman who had told his fortune when he was a boy. Sounds barmy, doesn't it? I couldn't invent anything as daft as that. And it gets even dafter. That idiot brother of mine reckoned he found the very same booth in this arcade exactly where it had been way back. I know you're probably thinking what I did: but that's what he said.'

'But it wasn't the same woman though. Well it wouldn't be. The old girl Rob described to me yonks ago would have been well past her century by now, I reckon. Apparently these days somebody else is doing the same sort of thing but now she's Mystic Maggie. Obviously she'd moved along with the times.'

'What Rob wanted was confirmation of the original reading he'd been given, or something entirely different. Instead of playing it canny and paying up and seeing what the woman came up with as a new reading for a new customer, the idiot told her exactly why he'd come and gave her all the details of what Leona had told him back in the seventies. As soon as she heard the name *Leona* she became very dismissive and said that anything she'd been told by 'that old fraud' was a load of nonsense and a pack of lies. She told Rob about the age-old feud between two Romany families; hers and Leona's, and if he wanted the real truth – it could only come from her. Anything else was worthless. Rob came out of her booth a few quid lighter in his pocket but with a smile on his face. He now had a long, happy life to look forward to.'

'I ask you? Is it just me, or had he lost it? Apparently what convinced Rob she was on the up and up was the fact that she told him he was unmarried – a bloke living on his own. You wouldn't need a crystal ball to work that out. Anyone with an IQ in double figures just had to look at Rob to know by looking at him there was no woman in his life. You know how he looked – untidy and always needing a haircut. Anyway, whatever she said seemed to cheer him up.'

'End of story you'd think. Not quite. When Rob died last year the police came round that night. They'd traced me as next of kin and I was needed to identify the body. I went along and I hope it's something I hope none of you ever have to do. Not nice at all.'

'There was one especially weird thing. The police gave me whatever he had with him when he died and in his wallet he still had that piece of paper he'd shown me thirty-odd years before. Same paper: same spelling mistake.'

'I went to the Inquest of course. They had a witness who saw it all. The way he told it was that he was hiding in a bus-shelter keeping out of the cloudburst. He said he'd never seen rain as heavy. He saw a car going through all the water on the road – like going through a ford he said – throwing up bow waves as if it was a boat at sea. It splashed this bloke – Rob that was – almost like throwing buckets of water over him. Rob jumped back, slipped and skidded into this scaffolding that was against a building. He banged his head, very hard. The doctor said he must have died instantly. This witness also said something that I won't ever forget. What he said was that *'The rain probably caused it with water in the electrics but the traffic lights at the junction were going on and off like Blackpool Illuminations at the time.'*

'So there you have it. Rob was forty-five when he died – actually two days short of his forty-sixth birthday – and you know what I said about the comments at the inquest with the water and the flashing lights. Was the old gipsy right or was it all coincidence? I don't know and probably never will. An explanation that makes sense? I can't give one. Perhaps one of you lot can?'

We looked at each other and shook our heads. No, we couldn't. Not a single explanation between us. So I got a round in, Pete lit yet another cigarette, and we all stood around, deep in our separate thoughts.

A SINGLE RED ROSE.

(Published in *Fiction on the Web.* November 2013).

It rained heavily the night we met Gordon. We were at the *Beijing* when it began and rather than get soaked going back to our apartment we decided to linger over an extra drink until it stopped.

This chap was at the next table and he seemed to be putting off leaving just as we were. We didn't know him, but his efforts at trying to talk Sinshe into giving him her telephone number earlier had made quite an entertaining little side-show that kept the customers in earshot amused.

Sinshe is a charming girl, tall for a Chinese, well liked by all, and part of the pleasure of eating in her restaurant is the welcome she gives everyone – a smile from ear to ear and kisses on both cheeks. She giggles a lot, probably to cover the embarrassment she feels at the language limitation. If you bump into her anywhere down in La Corumba, in the bank or market for instance, or on the street, anywhere in the town, you get the same greeting.

Well, on this particular evening this man who turned out to be Gordon was getting nowhere. He clearly had very little Spanish and Sinshe has what I think of as 'menu English' – so he was stymied. She knew what he was after, of course, but it was all harmless fun. He didn't know what we knew, of course, that she's married and has a young son. And the man in the kitchen – you can't really call him the chef – might be her husband for all we know. Burly too and big for a Chinese bloke.

This chap Gordon was alone and clearly wanted to chat. It turned out that he is in the antiques trade and regularly drives through France and into Spain, going south through the Costas as far as Gibraltar and then he heads up into Portugal on the return journey, doing deals on the way. La Corumba, it seems, is one of his occasional stops. He has a 'chum' – very wealthy, Gordon said – who has a flash villa inland at Boronda el Tillos and Gordon stays there whenever he's in the area. This friend is away at present so Gordon was trying his luck for the night with Sinshe.

We were in the antiques game ourselves for many years back in the UK and know our way round the business, so with some shared background we had a pleasant chat. Knowing what we know from the inside, we could see through his tales. He wasn't telling lies – just exaggerating. Every deal was a winner, and he never made any mistakes in his trading. Of course this is all nonsense. Everyone in the trade slips up sometimes — whatever they might say — buying the wrong piece, missing seeing some damage or paying too much for something. Even the best aren't infallible.

His over the top way of telling how well he had done didn't bother us in the least as he was so like scores of people we've met over the years. Both sexes, all ages and nationalities – everyone has a tale to tell – all you have to remember is to divide everything you are told by two and you begin to approach the truth.

I remembered meeting a lady who had for some years run a B & B place somewhere on the South coast back in England – her comment seemed apt for Gordon. What she said was *'In my time here I've met many retired bank managers but I've yet to meet the man who was a retired bank-clerk.'*

Gordon, we concluded, had told his tales so often that he had convinced himself of their truth and assumed his listeners believed him. In other words, he wasn't certain any more what was true and what was false. A nice enough fellow but not necessarily one to do business with. The sort who probably would have made a successful politician. All froth and no beer.

You've probably seen that chap *'Lovejoy'* on the television – an antiques dealer who is scruffy, untidy and a bit of a sartorial mess. Much more typical of blokes we'd known who live the life Gordon leads – a life that involves a lot of time on the road and probably some occasional sleeping rough in the back of a van. Gordon, though, could have been at *The Dorchester Antiques Fair* on Park Lane and not looked out of place. When we met him he was dressed to suit Spain – not Bond Street – but everything he wore was spot on.

Top quality clothes and shoes, one of those frustrating hair styles that we lesser mortals with little hair left can merely dream of and never actually have – you know the sort: the hair is always at just the right stage of growth between visits to the barber and is never obviously overdue for cutting – Prince Charles is the same. Gordon's hair was very dark and thick too – damn him – and was parted on the right, the side that I always associate with Conservative MP's and ex-public schoolboys. Tall, early-twenties, good looking – or so Charlotte reckoned – and with an upper crust accent he seemed to be one of these people the fairy blessed at birth with a head-start over the rest of us lesser beings.

If he did have a problem we suspected he was a little short of the readies. Despite all his tales of deals done and won, a few comments in the conversation hinted at a man slightly down on his luck but hiding his lack of cash very well.

When you've been sharing everything, good and bad, for as long as Charlotte and I have, just a look tells me all I need to know about her views on life at any particular moment. Certainly if she is unhappy, then I can sense that in no time, so on this particular evening I knew all was well. There was none of the usual body language that, without a word being spoken, lets me know when she's had enough and it's time to go, so with us both happy I just allowed the conversation to continue.

To be honest I think Charlotte was a little infatuated with our companion – especially when he moved to our table and sat directly opposite her. My wife isn't a drinker – the odd glass of wine is enough, but that evening she was enjoying herself and when she popped off to the loo I ordered another bottle of Rioja. I don't normally drink wine myself so it was all for her – she must have noticed but chose not to comment. Well, I might need to help her finish the bottle – it's always a shame to waste it.

The conversation drifted on to people in and around La Corumba. By now we know quite a number – mostly Brits, of course – and when Gordon asked us if we knew his friend Robin Matlock-Fowler we were able to recognise him from the description. We remembered seeing him in another local restaurant, very pricey and up-market, sitting at a table that had a reserved sign on it. Twice now, Charlotte reminded me.

My memory isn't great these days but I can remember faces quite well. He was rather like Gordon now that I think about it – tall, very good looking and with longish hair, blonde in Robin's case – and clearly just as concerned with his appearance as Gordon was. A man with an eye for the ladies too I remember thinking. The red rose buttonhole in a white linen jacket was a touch flash for a small Spanish coastal town but he seemed able to carry it off.

I mentioned to Gordon that his friend Robin seemed to have a female companion with him each time we saw him and I thought that it wasn't always the same one. Gordon nodded and we settled back as Gordon began to tell us more about his friend.

'Robin,' he said, 'is another of my chums from prep-school and we both started at Eton on the same day. So did Rupert too, as it happens. Rupert's the chap whose villa I'm staying in this weekend. We've all kept in touch over the years – we still move in the same circles and see friends and friends of friends and all that. I do know that Robin comes here occasionally but it's nothing more than coincidence that we have connections in La Corumba.'

'You say you've seen Robin with different women? Well, there's nothing new in that. Robin has always been a randy sod. I like the ladies too – you saw me trying it on with that Chinese waitress earlier – but Robin's really Premier League. His little red book would be worth a bomb if someone knew where he kept it. Never married – simply plays the field. Lives in London but travels a lot. Less than he used to – his people were *'Names'* at Lloyds and lost rather a lot of money – you probably read about it in the papers.'

It had all been big news a year or two back, and I'm sure Gordon's friends had their own viewpoint – but certainly in the less exalted circles we know better, there was no sympathy for the *'toffs who take every penny they can for years, then run whingeing to the media when the profits turn to losses'*. They're a cleaned up recollection of a friend's words – reflecting a widely held view. An apparently well-heeled couple had been in a discussion programme on the telly and complaining rather bitterly about their plight and claimed to have been *'wiped out'*. This was the first time I had heard the phrase used like this and it came up again the evening we met Gordon. Their tales of woe brought little sympathy from my friend and their pleas for *'someone to do something for them'* really got him going.

'Probably down to their second-last manor house in Kent, I expect.' Restrained words from Peter, a highly successful self-made businessman with abrasive opinions on bureaucracy and interfering government departments. We didn't comment and just let Gordon carry on.

'The *'Names'* business hit Robin badly. He personally had no direct financial involvement but his parents had, and they were pretty well wiped out'. There's that phrase again.

'Before this, Robin's future life had had been mapped out for him. He knew he would have the lot when his old man kicked the bucket – he'd inherit the title – in itself being Lord Carsington means nothing but a title does still carry weight if one cares to use it to impress – and he'd simply do as little as poss until everything became his. I know I make him sound like a lazy oik but he did have a job - *'something in the city'* as they say – and as long as he could have a cheque from the family to top-up his income when he needed it he could just drift along until old Lord M – his pater – went upstairs to the House of Lords in the sky. Then everything changed and Robin had to think very seriously about his financial future.'

'We had a long chat about it when Robin realised how dodgy his situation had become. OK. – there was the title, of course – but the City these days isn't the place it used to be for nobs with a pedigree and not much else to offer. Just because a fellow went to a good school and his father was someone doesn't automatically open doors any more these days. Robin isn't thick – but he isn't a rocket scientist either.'

'His temperament also is a problem. Robin's one of those chaps who needs stimulation – the mental sort. He gets bored easily and can't settle to anything unless he feels it's a challenge. That ruled out a humdrum, routine job that didn't pay well and would bore the pants off him. He felt that anything like that was beneath him. Robin's a bit of a snob, truth to tell. It's almost inevitable when you consider how he was brought up.'

I ordered another drink for Gordon. Lottie was still nursing her wine and I switched to Diet Coke. Lottie signalled a warning at me – we both had noticed that Gordon was beginning to slur his words and his face was becoming flushed. He had been drinking before we arrived and while he was with us he had a couple of extra drinks while we sat and sipped ours. We already knew he was going to his local base by taxi later so that was safely taken care of. Normally by this stage we would have long gone, but we wanted to hear more about his friend Robin.

'Basically Robin has two things really going for him. Charm by the bucketful and he appeals to the ladies, bless 'em. He can charm the birds off a tree and the girls can't resist him. What he does nowadays is to use his biggest assets – charm and sex appeal – to live. When you saw him recently having a meal in here Robin was at work.'

'He has a routine that goes like this. He places an advert in the English language papers here in the Costas. This is a normal enough contact type thing, men looking for women and women looking for fellas – you see columns in the press like this everywhere these days – and he collects all his answers together, groups them by region, Costa Blanca, Costa del Sol and so on – and goes up and down the coast to meet ladies from those he selects. Naturally he's very choosy and careful.'

Charlotte looked across at me. I didn't look back but I felt the beginning of a change in her opinion of Gordon. She has some very strong views on some things and sensed the direction the monologue was heading and didn't like it.

He went on, clearly unaware of his audience's reactions. 'Many of the people who advertise would tell you they're looking for companionship or friendship – which is often a euphemism for sex – but they won't admit it. Not all, of course by any means – many people are genuinely looking for a companion to share a lonely life – poor sods. In Robin's case his main concern is money. If it's clear the woman wants sex and as Robin put it to me *'If she's not one of the Ugly Sisters and needs a sack over her face'* he'll oblige. That side of it is merely incidental as Robin can have his pick of almost any young dollies he meets.'

Gordon looked across at us. 'When you saw him, were the women 'of mature years' as the phrase politely puts it?'

Sensing that Charlotte might have strong words to say to our companion once she did speak, I jumped in before she could reply.

'Well you must remember, Gordon, that we've seen him twice or three times only as far as we know, but 'yes' – both times they were. As far as I can remember the first one we saw was probably in her mid forties and the second one much older – in her sixties I reckon. Well preserved, though, for a 'mature' woman.'

I decided to press home the point. 'So, your friend chooses the older women rather than the bimbos – no doubt, they've more money, but what's his ploy then? Obviously it's a scam but how does he work it?'

I was keeping a watchful eye on my wife. Clearly Gordon wasn't an overly sensitive soul – most people would have been aware of her rapidly changing mood by now – even though she had listened without intervening so far. Not only the basic concept was upsetting her but the increasingly sexist bias in his tone was getting through to her.

As Charlotte is herself well into her sixties some of the comments about *'well preserved'* and *'mature women'* were rather too near home for not to be aware of them. Her increasingly angry reactions and body language were like water off a duck's back to Gordon as he continued in the same vein.

'You're right there, of course. He assumed the older birds' – Charlotte was near to exploding by now –'had the money but his ploy for getting his hands on some of it was simple enough. The way he explained it to me was like this........'

'........Imagine you're a woman – let's be kind and say you're not in the first flush of youth. Not necessarily 'mutton dressed as lamb' but close to it. Assume you're meeting Robin at a prearranged time and place. You turn up – don't forget your date will be a complete stranger to you – there's a reserved table for two with a very good looking, well dressed young man waiting for you. He will be wearing a red rose – as arranged – greets you with a kiss on the hand and presents you with a single rose all the time talking in a posh accent. She'll think Christmas has come early, won't she?'

'This gorgeous chap begins with an apology. He wanted to present you with a bouquet – he mentions orchids – but sadly, it can only be a single flower this evening. Why? Because that very day he has been robbed and most of his ready money has been stolen along with credit cards, driving licence, passport and a few other things. In fact, he ought at this moment to be on his way to the Police Station to give them details of the robbery, but that would have meant letting his guest down and in no way would he consider doing this on their first meeting, etc, etc, etc.'

'It also meant that for this, *'their first meeting'* – the merest hint here of something beyond that particular evening we both thought was a clever touch – sadly he could pay only for himself. Until he sorted out something with the bank on Monday morning there was no way he could act as the host and all that implied. He was ashamed and embarrassed to say it, but the lady would have to pay for her own meal and drinks.'

'I don't expect to have to spell it out. Most of these old birds by now had stars in their eyes with all the old-fashioned courtesy and charm from this young man with the film star looks and they became like putty in his hands. Brilliant scheme, isn't it?'

Neither of us replied. Lottie made violent signs to catch Sinshe's eye for the bill.

Gordon continued. 'Where the evenings go from there he played by ear. Sometimes Robin would finish up in bed with some woman old enough to be his mother, sometimes it ended there and then with the occasional 'client' smelling a rat. Normally money would change hands – purely a loan of course – then Robin would have maybe one more 'Exploratory Business Meal' as he called them in the town, then he would move on.'

'He always has to be careful not to overdo an area and slip up that way. There's some sort of filing system involved somewhere – there must be. I suppose he uses a computer. He's one of those guys who know about PC's and stuff like that. Robin's so much better at that sort of thing than I am. I'm sure I'd slip up if I ever tried to do it and I would date the same woman twice or something stupid like that.'

To me Gordon was looking more and more pathetic – a sad figure of a man on a steepening downhill slope. His earlier attempted portrayal of easy superiority and control was gone – a veneer little thicker than paper was going by the minute. A man who clearly wasn't overly blessed with brains was becoming even more stupid as he drank.

'What you really mean is that he is a con-man and a gigolo. And you think it's all very clever.'

This was Charlotte. She was struggling to control herself and managing it well – certainly better than I thought she would. So many people shout and rant when they are angry but Lottie kept her voice down and her protest was all the more powerful because of it.

'What you've told us is as mean a trick as any I've heard. It's disgusting.'

'And so are you Gordon. Early in the evening I thought you were OK but not now. If you encourage 'friends' like that you're nearly as bad as he is.' When she said *'friends'* there was real contempt in her voice.

'I want to go home, Charles – rain or not. Now.'

Gordon seemed taken aback. His arrogance had stopped him noticing what anyone with normal feelings would have grasped much earlier, and even when his partially fuddled mind sensed all was not well, he still underestimated the strength of her feelings. He turned to Charlotte.

'I'm sorry, my dear' – a phrase he shouldn't have used to Charlotte with the mood she was in – 'you feel like that and I can understand why. Any comments I made about Robin that seemed in favour of his tricks were simply respect for the cleverness of the scheme. I didn't say I approved and there is no way that I would ever do anything like it. He and I are old chums but we do have different standards.' By now the words were slurred and almost tailed off at this point.

'Spineless wimp' were the words that came into my mind as Gordon wriggled on the hook of his own making.

I felt I had to say something to show support with my wife so I mumbled something or other vaguely disapproving about the whole affair, paid the bill and we left, having turned down an offer to meet up the next day for a drink.

Clearly Gordon was too drunk to fully understand all that he was saying, and unable to grasp that he was telling strangers that his friend was a criminal. Completely sober I would have been strongly opposed to the scheme and its deviousness and undoubtedly would have said so. As it was I should have but didn't, and next morning wasn't proud of the wishy-washy line I had taken.

Neither of us felt that Gordon really understood our disapproval. Lottie was all for going to the police and reporting Robin as a fraudster but having slept on it we decided to leave it alone. My feeling was that eventually Robin would be caught and having a friend like Gordon would make it sooner rather than later.

***

Sinshe gave us a special welcome when we called in one evening several months later – our first visit after we got back to Spain the following October. We had our usual seat on the side-wall and noticed a reserved sign on the next table.

'Do you think Robin's back to his old tricks?' Charlotte whispered.

A figure appeared from the passageway leading to the toilets. It was Gordon. He was wearing a splendid black blazer of a shiny, silky material, grey trousers and had a red rose in his buttonhole. He could have stepped from the pages of a fashion magazine. Just before he sat down he saw us and came over.

'Hello, you two. Good to see you both. Can't stop to chat, my date's due any moment. I've set up in opposition to Robin. I'm making my debut tonight – wish me luck. Tell you about it later – she's just coming in.'

We looked towards the door where a lady was being led by Sinshe to Gordon's table. In her late-fifties, we both thought afterwards when we compared notes. Tallish, with good features and a minimum of make-up, good dress sense, and we agreed, clearly a lady with taste.

Their table was near enough for us to see and hear what was going on, but after the initial greeting and the presentation of the solitary rose by Gordon to his guest and the prepared story of the robbery and how it left him with a problem, there was no-one in the room who could have failed to hear what happened next.

The lady, a Mrs. Clayton as she had been addressed, rose to her feet and took a jug of water that she poured over Gordon's head. We heard her calling Gordon a *'con-man and rogue',* there were references to his *'smoothie friend', 'do you think I'm stupid enough to fall for the same trick twice?'* and *'your crooked associate still owes me 200 euros and I want it back'.*

Sinshe by now was hovering at the table, obviously uncertain what to do and her limited English stopping her from sorting out the dispute. Mrs. Clayton turned to her and, in fluent Spanish, asked Sinshie to call the police. At this Gordon made a dash for the door, managing to burst past a customer who made an unsuccessful grab for him, and ran out on to the street. Two uniformed Guardia arrived a few minutes later and took statements from Mrs. Clayton but that seemed to end the matter as far as they were concerned. They lingered over drinks that Sinshe gave them until their radios squawked and off they went.

We introduced ourselves to Mrs. Clayton − a charming lady as it turned out – invited her to join us for a drink and told her what Gordon had told us those months previously. It added little really to what she knew – other than Robin's father's title, if that were true − but she was hoping to track down either or both of them and was prepared to spend time and money if needed. She appeared to have plenty of both and seemed to relish the challenge.

All three of us agreed that any aspiring con-man who failed on his first attempt shouldn't be hard to find. Somehow Lottie and I felt that Gordon had to fail on his personal Day One – anything else would somehow be out of character for a man clearly destined to be one of life's losers.

***

As far as we were concerned that ended our involvement with Gordon and his 'chum' Robin. We saw neither of them again but did come across an item in the *Costa Blanca News* a year or so later. Actually it was the photograph of Mrs. Clayton that Charlotte saw and recognised. It seems that she was as good as her word.

She had traced them as far as Almeria, further down the coast in Spain, and had managed to have both of them arrested. There was a string of offences listed and dozens of victims had complained. Robin – whose real name was George Herring (27) - and Gordon (Mason) (25) were given eighteen months and twelve months prison respectively and on release were to be handed over to the UK police for investigation of further offences.

We contacted Mrs. Clayton through the paper and congratulated her. She sent us an interesting letter back in which she said that the time spent on tracking down the two had been among the most interesting part of her life since her husband had died some years before. A real battleaxe but very likeable.

Reading between the lines we think that she must have had what they call 'hands on' contact with the detective agency she employed. A sort of *'Money's no object – just go out and find them. And I want a twice a week update, too'* approach.. We felt that the two men had no chance once Mrs. C was involved.

One bit of news she did pass on. Robin / George blamed Gordon for his problems and they had a fight in prison. Neither was seriously hurt but apparently extra time was added to their sentences – something that pleased Mrs. C. no end. In addition to that they had – foolishly, but in character – managed to upset some of the real hard men on the inside with the inevitable reprisals. We gathered that their good looks had been somewhat diminished by the beatings they were given.

Mrs. Clayton also told us that she sent a single red rose to each of them once a month and she would keep doing that until their removal back to England. She didn't seem surprised when they didn't reply to thank her. She carried on sending them anyway. They're due out later this year. Somehow I don't think they've heard the last of Mrs. Clayton.

SHARON.

(Published in *Winamop.* February 2015.)

I'd like to tell you about a young woman I know – Sharon Jennings, her name is. She's a neighbour and has been since she was a baby. She lives in the same tower block as I do – two doors away on the eighth floor. I enjoy my privacy, so I won't say exactly where that is except it's in south London.

I like Sharon, and her mother, Sheila. I've become a sort of substitute father to the family – a bit more like a grandfather really. There's a younger sister, Kylie, but I'm sorry to say she shows signs of going wrong at a young age. Sharon's fine, though. Those sociology people who do these things would have her down as a *'no-hoper'* – *'minimum potential material'* or something like that in that jargon they use. Their files would have all the boxes ticked – brought up by a single parent; living where she does they would expect her to be on drugs; bullied at school, probably a drop-out from there as well, pregnant in her 'teens, and later either in a dead-end job or living off benefits. They've been proved wrong on pretty well everything and no-one is more pleased than me about it. Let me tell you some more.

Sharon was a happy child. At thirteen or so when my tale begins, no-one could find anything to dislike about her. Plain, bespectacled and plump with straight, straggly hair, the girls at the Thomas Round Comprehensive didn't see her as a challenge with the boys so they didn't bully her. Sharon was well aware of boys but they didn't seem to be aware of her except as just one of the gang, and a pal who happened to be female. A friendly outgoing teenager, usually one of a crowd, avoiding all the pitfalls the experts said were lying in wait for her.

If there was a problem with Sharon, it was one shared by all the kids she knocked about with, and was as much down to the world we live in as anything else. That was their obsession with what they called 'celebrity.' People I'd never heard of were their idols and they lived and dreamed other people's lives. I can't understand it personally but then I'm not their age. Sharon was just like the others, and forever seemed to have copies of magazines writing about the doings of these people who meant so much to her. As individuals and as a group the peak of ambition was to become famous – to be in the papers or to be on the telly. It didn't seem to matter what for. Just being famous – that's all. I find it all rather sad.

In school she wasn't stupid, but certainly wasn't academic and her results consistently put her at the bottom end of her class. But, and it's a big 'but', when she showed me the reports every term every single one said something nice about her and her behaviour.

***

'Unique' is a much misused word but our Sharon was just that at the Thomas Round School. Nobody could match her record for attendance. Right from day one in the First Year Sharon had turned up for school every single day. Sometimes with colds, once with a sprained ankle when she hobbled in on a stick, and even when there was a bug of some sort going the rounds that gave most of the others in her class an excuse for a couple of days off — Sharon went to school. Quite an achievement – and I know her mum Sheila was very proud of her.

There was a teacher at Thomas Round, Jonathan Pilkington his name was, a likeable young chap, who had taken a shine to Sharon. No, not in that way – Jonty had his own steady boy-friend – but he saw something in her and tried to encourage young Sha to develop what he felt was in there somewhere. He taught the kids some of the basics of computers and also tried to interest them in his own hobby of photography. Apparently he had all the proper gear at home, lenses, dark-rooms, tripods, developing tanks – stuff I know next to nothing about – and he allowed the class to see some of it sometimes; in end of term lessons and that sort of thing.

Then one day he brought in a couple of those new digital cameras that were all the rage then and becoming more popular by the week. He gave all the kids a few goes each and allowed them to take pictures of whatever they wanted – almost inevitably most of the pictures were of the children snapping each other. Then with his Computer Teacher's hat on he showed the class what he could do when he put the images into the PC gismo – something else I don't know much about – and did things with them to turn them into better pictures. The kids were fascinated and I can imagine that, knowing them as I did, quite a few of the lads were wondering where they could steal a camera from, or if they had to pay for one, who they could mug to get the money.

Sharon joined in with the others and took a few pictures but it was what the teacher and his computer could do with this basic material that impressed her most. She was so thrilled as she told me about it, and I was delighted that she'd found something she could do and enjoyed doing. It must have been obvious to Mr. Pilkington too, as a few days later he gave Sharon a camera. It was one of the very first digitals that had come on to the market, inevitably Japanese, and already out of date as this week's top of the range model became obsolete by next Wednesday. No more use to him it but to Sharon it was a dream come true.

She took it to school with her – despite warnings from her mum, me and apparently Mr. Pilkington too. Once she realised there was no film to buy and she could re-use whatever took the pictures inside the camera she was over the moon. Every spare moment Sharon was out snapping away at something or other. The teacher was a real brick. He stayed behind after school whenever Sha had photo'd anything and put it through the computer. Then as Sharon learned, he allowed her to doctor the pictures herself – and any that were special he let her print out in colour for us to see.

November came and there was a freakish spot of early snow: Sharon managed to snap a robin eating from a hanging net of nuts the kids at the school had put out. Beginner's luck or what, it was a smashing picture. The bird with its brilliant red breast against the snowy background, it really was lovely. It could have been a proper Christmas card. Between them the two 'cropped' the picture – their word, not mine – and framed it. Oh, Sha was so pleased.

Things went on from there. Jonathan e-mailed the picture off to the local paper and they printed it in all its full colour in the

special *'Yuletide Post'* edition. They sent a young woman reporter round to interview Sharon who became tongue-tied, so Jonty and the reporter concocted something nice to go with the two photos they printed – Sharon and her robin picture. Sha became very emotional and tearful.

Not everyone welcomed what had happened. Inevitably there was a degree of jealousy that ended in Sharon's camera being stolen. Everyone thought they knew who did it – one girl's name came up regularly – but, without proof, the investigation got nowhere.

Sharon wasn't camera-less for long. At the final assembly before the Christmas holiday the Headmaster made an announcement that to mark the *'wonderful and unequalled attendance record'* (his words) *'Sharon Jennings is to receive a special award.'* It may appear a bit corny and perhaps obvious but Sharon was given a new digital camera. '*With even more pixels than Mr. Pilkington has.'* The Headmaster always had fancied himself as a bit of a wag.

The *Post* printed another article about Sharon and her new camera – using much of the same material as before. Whether or not the publicity was to blame nobody knows, but the new *Muji 549F* was stolen on Boxing Day from Sharon as she was out taking photographs of the queue at the local *B & Q* Sale.

Sharon was distraught. Her mother and I talked about replacing the stolen item for her, but we couldn't afford to. So Sharon was left with memories, a particularly lovely photograph and lots of other decent ones on the school computer, and the beginnings of a scrapbook of newspaper cuttings – but no camera.

Somehow, even though it was the holiday, the news reached Jonathan Pilkington. Clearly he knew people who knew people and had contacts, and within days Sharon was called to the local branch of *Comet*. There she was greeted by the Area Manager and the store management, the same young woman from the local press – and a 'stringer', I believe they call him, from the *Sun* – and left an hour or so later with a replacement camera that exactly matched the one just stolen, and lots of accessories and bits and pieces all donated by well-wishers. I was with Sha and her mum and it wasn't only those two who were wiping back tears that day.

Sharon's story was in the nationals over the next couple of days and two more reporters came out to interview her. By then she was becoming a little less nervous in her responses but still came over as a likeable, unassuming schoolgirl. She had even become confident enough to take off her glasses when she was being photographed. Her scrapbook was becoming quite bulky by now but her mum and me did our best to keep her feet on the ground. Fortunately it wasn't too difficult. She was still our Sha.

***

By now Sharon's lot were in their final year. She was still down near the bottom of the class, still never missing a day and still busy taking photographs of everything that interested her. Mr. Pilkington was giving her advice still, but that was more on the computer side than on the picture-taking aspect. Her mini-celebrity was now a thing of the past and any resentment due to her few weeks of prominence had almost gone. Big plans were being made by all the youngsters in their search for fame and fortune, and those that couldn't even dream of the heights were beginning to think of life in the real world.

It was three weeks before the end of term and the final year children had the day off while some of the juniors were taking their exams – and as Sharon said – *'on those days they want all the teachers they can spare for watching and invigorating. They won't stop the cribbing but they're trying to keep it down.'* Yes, *'invigorating'* was the word she used. I hadn't the heart to correct her – it was probably the longest word I'd ever heard her use.

Sharon was patrolling down on the Broadway, with the inevitable *Muji* in her hand. She'd taken a handful of photographs, more for something to do – as she said *'nothing special and probably for deletion later on.'* She was clicking away at a traffic warden arguing with an *Escort* driver just as two men ran out of the *National Westminster Bank.* Brushing aside a man delivering next door, they dashed for a white van, taking off their masks as they did so. The instant they were in the van, it pulled away, knocking a cyclist off his bike as they went. Sharon managed to take three pictures and she was checking their quality as the first police car arrived.

The men were arrested two hours later and all the money recovered. Sharon's photographs didn't help in the arrest – the police had already had a tip-off and knew where to look for the gang. Her pictures were just extra confirmation of the men's identities. As the arrests were already made the photos were not needed by the authorities. Instead they were in the papers next morning with headlines like '*Plonkers'* (The *Mirror*) and '*How thick can you get?'* (The *Sun*) – both papers making fun of thieves who uncovered their faces in a crowded High Street.

She didn't know which was better – the generous cheques or seeing her name on the front page of National papers. Sharon felt just then she really was on the way to becoming a professional photographer. More for her scrapbook. The bank sent Sharon a small cheque and invited her and her mum to a presentation. The Police called her in and presented Miss Sharon Jennings with a Citizen's Commendation. Then Sharon left school.

Jonathan and the Headmaster made a few phone calls and Sha was offered, and jumped at, a job in the local *PCWorld* – in the section selling digital cameras. She wasn't brilliant at it, but her likeability and enthusiasm helped her make a few sales – and she qualified for staff discount on her occasional purchases.

***

Now a few years on from those days Sharon – still at *PCWorld*, still living at home and still taking pictures right, left and centre – has lost some of her puppy fat, wears contacts instead of her old specs and turned into an attractive young woman, attractive enough to have a steady boy friend – one I'm pleased to say I approve of. She's had no more strokes of good fortune and life has settled into a predictable routine for her. Whatever happens, even if it's nothing special ever again, Sharon has had her touch of glory and celebrity – partly proving that weird-looking American bloke with the funny name was right when he talked about '*Everybody being famous for fifteen minutes.'*

One final point. There's now a *Sharon Jennings Attendance Prize* at Thomas Round School waiting to be won by someone. It will be given to the first pupil who manages to equal Sharon's record of never missing a single day's school in his or her time there. Somehow I don't think the prize will ever be won. That's good for Sha but sad in a way as she'd been told that she would present the award personally to the winner. And that would have meant another photograph from the local paper to go into her scrap book.

MR. SMITH'S PROMOTION.

(Published in *Winamop*. June 2014).

Monday morning. The office had slipped into its unhurried routine – hushed voices, rustling paper, the occasional ring of a telephone and already – after less than thirty minutes at their desks – anticipation of the tea-trolley. Over on the left near one of the windows Pete and Frank were having their usual post-weekend inquest on Saturday's game. It was the only point of real animation among the twenty people in the room, several of whom were day-dreaming and already looking forward to Friday evening. Nowhere were there signs of people hard at work, dedicated to helping their employer's business succeed better due to their efforts. Newspaper editorials and Government exhortation spoke of the 'work ethic', and 'export or die' was a phrase heard a lot back then – but no sign of it was apparent in an over-warm, comfortably furnished office.

For this was the early nineteen-fifties and everyone in the three sections that made up the Cost Office knew that jobs were plentiful, dismissals were virtually unheard of and no-one need try too hard. 'You'd have to rape the Chairman's daughter to be sacked from here these days' as one of them put it, then added 'and have you seen the Chairman's daughter?' Certainly the younger clerks knew they could leave on Friday if they chose and be in work again within days. Only the few older men, with thoughts and plans firmly focussed on pensions and retirement, showed any form of interest or dedication to their employer. That is except for two men, sitting next to each other in the third row of desks. Each had his head down, apparently diligently applying himself to the pile of papers on his desk.

The two were Harold Smith and Sidney Jardine. Not that these first names were in common use in the office – and most certainly neither would address the other by using them. There was a feud between the two and each was formally *'Mister Smith'* or *'Mister Jardine'* when either spoke to, or of the other. This was soon noticed by the others and in the office generally they were normally referred to as *'Mister Tweedledum and Mister Tweedledee'* with the two names being interchangeable. The names were almost inevitably from the office wags, especially Ken on the back row and young Arthur, the office boy. Young Arthur seemed never to be stuck for words about what he saw and heard around him, and his irreverent comments were usually regarded as apt, often funny, but sometimes going just too far. So, every now and then, young Arthur was gently reprimanded and reminded about showing more respect for his more senior colleagues. All very discreet and gentle, and just a minor ritual of its time that everyone recognised as such and ignored. After all, standards had to be maintained in this new, modern, post-war world.

The *Tweedledum and Tweedledee* names were apt. Even the most straight-laced old fogey in the office had to admit that. *'Like a pair of bookends'* was another comment, made as they stood there together, flanking the young woman from the Personnel Department who brought them up to their new home. Similar in height and build, both short and a little overweight, both around the fifty mark, clean-shaven, thinning grey hair liberally covered with grease carefully positioned to try to cover a shining scalp and both men customarily wearing the standard office uniform of the day – three-piece suits in dark grey with a subdued striped tie, plain white shirt, and highly polished shoes. Even the horn-rimmed spectacles looked interchangeable.

They had arrived at the office about three months before. It was soon obvious that something was amiss between the two and that they had known each other previously. Whatever the problem was between them, they brought it with them, but whether they expected to be sitting just a foot or so from the other is very doubtful, and the rigid layout of the desks didn't allow any evasive action by either man. So, like new starters in offices the world over, they dutifully sat where they were placed, and then tried to ignore each other as far as they could.

New people moving into an established environment everywhere are watched – sometimes openly, sometimes not. Whichever way their new colleagues studied them, either blatantly or surreptitiously, the chilly atmosphere between the men couldn't be missed. Neither man showed any inclination to become close to anyone else in the office, so no confidences were exchanged and everyone was left wondering just what it was all about. Even Edward, a long-time bachelor and known by all as a tireless gossip failed to find out the cause of the feud. 'Give me time, give me time. If there's a story there, then you all know Teddy won't let you down.'

***

The man who should have put an end to nonsense like this was Mr. Mathews. He was their Section Leader and their direct superior but his view – never stated but clear – was *'that as long as it doesn't interfere with the running of the Section – why interfere?'* Young Arthur had noticed this and came up with the name of *'Nelson'* for Mr. Mathews. He used the term one day to old Mr. Foster, a man generally believed to be over a hundred and as he was always first in the office and last away, thought by some to sleep overnight at his desk. Whether he did or not, as was his way he gently reminded Arthur of his lowly perch at the bottom of the pecking order, and then soon afterwards explained to Miss Fothersgill, allegedly almost as old, just how the term had originated with the great Admiral himself and the telescope to his blind eye. 'Nelson' Mathews himself meanwhile had his thoughts on other and higher things. His mind and devotions were elsewhere.

Mr. Matthews was Section Head of his small group in the office. He did little work and had minimal responsibilities − something that was obvious to everyone else. With a powerful supporter in the Chief Accountant, Mathews' colleagues had found all they could do was grumble among themselves and accept the situation. Undemanding as his work-load was, it had been decreed that he needed two assistant clerks, so creating the vacancies filled by Mr. Smith and Mr. Jardine.

Status dictated that Mr. Matthews had a large desk by the window and next to the radiator. On the desk were two telephones – the second one allowing him to dial outside directly without going through the switchboard. His two clerks each had smaller desks with a narrow gap between them and no telephone.

***

Many men have secret passions, but Mr. Matthews made no secret of his. He was a golf fanatic. He played at every conceivable opportunity and was Secretary of the local Club that he ran from his office desk, which had on it a framed photograph of himself following a hole-in-one at the 15th.

The Club was a popular one and there was a lengthy waiting list, but when a new Chief Accountant arrived he became a member almost immediately. By a remarkably fortunate and unlikely coincidence, Mr. Matthews had discovered an opening and he was able to add a powerful and valuable ally to the Club membership.

Mr. Matthews also ran the Company's Golfing Society. Regular inter-departmental games were arranged, and the latest project involved a match with the Company's major customer in Wales.

If these games were not played during the working week, then Mr. Matthews felt he had failed his colleagues. So, if golf-playing staff members were absent now and then, others not in the *'Magic Circle'*, as it became known to resentful non-golfing colleagues – or golfers who were not selected – had to realise that these mid-week matches were '*good for business and the Company stood to benefit from all the goodwill generated.'* This raised a few cynical eyebrows.

His priorities in the office were well established. Golf, then whatever workload was left a distant second. What did remain was delegated to his two assistants. Neither Mr. Smith nor Mr. Jardine played golf.

***

Mr. Smith was a keen gardener. A shaved lawn and rigorously controlled roses showed a degree of obsession but that was what he wanted. His special pride was an apple tree that he nursed and cared for like a baby, a tree which rewarded him each year with a rich crop of delicious fruit.

It was a tree with a problem, though. It had been planted by a previous owner near the privet hedge that marked the boundary between the house and the one next door. Years of prevailing wind and a lack of support early in its life had resulted in a mature tree that leaned, and grew with many of its branches overhanging the neighbour's garden.

Then Mr. Jardine moved into No 14 Acacia Avenue. Soon afterwards a large ginger cat started to be seen near Mr. Smith's roses. As the cat always came from that side, he assumed it belonged to his new neighbour, and a sighting of the creature scratching away in his flower beds one Saturday morning caused an angry and increasingly heated quarrel between the two. Only after another neighbour claimed ownership of the cat did Mr. Smith make a grudging apology.

The previous occupant of No 14 had accepted some tasty apples as compensation for part of his garden being put into deep shade by someone else's tree. Mr. Jardine curtly dismissed the offer of some Cox's –'They overhang my garden so they're mine anyway.'

Some days later a letter addressed to Mr. Jardine but with the wrong house number came through Mr. Smith's letter-box. He marked the letter *'Not known at this address'* and put it back into the post box. When it did reach Mr. Jardine several days later, he responded by cutting down those branches of the apple tree that overhung his garden.

The relationship between the two was now icy. As their paths crossed nowhere else, the friction between them was limited to being neighbours who did not get along.

Each could recognise his neighbour as one of the great tribe of office workers who lived in their dormitory suburb. They left home at the same time each morning to walk to the local Railway Station, boarded the same train taking them to City Central, then they went their own ways. One Monday morning they found themselves walking in the same direction and through the same door to start new jobs for the same Company in the same office on the same day. They found themselves with adjacent desks and the two had no option other than to work together.

***

Mr. Matthews had often said he would die happy if it was during a good round. Whether he was happy or not as he was about to drive off at his favourite 15th tee when he was hit on the temple by a wild shot from the 12th wasn't clear. He died instantly.

This happened on a Sunday morning. On the following Tuesday, Mr. Smith was part way through the *Daily Mail* crossword when he was summoned into the Cost Accountant's office.

'Sit down, Henry.'

Mr. Smith was slightly taken aback as he was unused to be addressed by anything other than 'Mr. Smith.'

'Actually, it's Harold, Sir.'

'Sorry, er... Harold. Shame about Peter, eh? He'll be sorely missed. Hard working chap with quite a future ahead of him. I went to see his wife – er, widow, yesterday, and she seems to be bearing up quite well. Brave little woman. I expect you know the funeral is on Thursday? I'll be going, of course, along with some of the Section Heads. The office must show the flag on this sad occasion.'

'No need for you to go, though, Henry. Someone has to keep the boat on course and the tiller steady.'

The Cost Accountant had a small boat moored near Ainsdale, and he tried to sail most weekends. Young Arthur had christened him *'Popeye.'*

'What I am going to say to you, I'll be saying to Stanley Jardine when he comes back from holiday. Next Monday, isn't it?' Mr. Smith nodded.

'Regarding the future for Waste Recovery and how it affects you, er...Horace. We won't be replacing Peter Matthews directly. You and.... er, Sidney, can manage between you, I'm sure. If you both work together I don't see any difficulty. Just take on that little bit extra each.

No problem there, is there? The extra duties will be so slight that there won't be any increase in salary, of course.'

He paused, leaned forward in his seat glancing to left and right even though there was no-one else in his office.

'I've heard whispers that you don't get on together, Herbert. Is that true? If there is a problem you can tell me about it. Try to forget I'm your boss here in the office. You can talk to me as man to man – in confidence, of course.'

Mr. Smith chose his words carefully.

'Your information is only partially correct, Sir. Any differences Mister Jardine and I may have don't get in the way of working together.'

'But I'm told you don't even speak to each other.'

'When it's to do with work we do converse, of course. The office always comes first. Socially we have nothing in common.'

'Well, quite frankly, I don't understand it, but I suppose you know your own business. As long as the Section doesn't suffer, that's what matters. Have you any questions then?'

Mr. Smith saw his opening and took it.

'Just about my position, Sir. That's all.'

'Your position? Haven't I just explained that? There's no change.'

'My position, Sir. My place in the Section.'

The Cost Accountant was clearly becoming more exasperated by the minute.

'I don't know what you're talking about. Don't waste my time like this. Spill it out, man.'

'The desk, Sir.'

'What desk. What are you going on about?'

'Mr. Matthews' desk. May I move to it and use it in future?'

'Oh, I see. Well, I suppose so. I can't see any reason why not. Yes, carry on. That's all for now, Henry.'

Mr. Smith was a happy man. Immediately on returning to the Section he began to empty the drawers of his old desk, and transferred his pens, paper, ruler and box of paper clips to their new home. Behind the desk, near the window was a coat rack with an empty coat hanger on it. He took off his jacket and put it on the hanger. The internal telephone rang.

'Waste Recovery Section – Mr. Smith speaking.' After answering the 'phone a quick look around revealed, disappointingly, that apparently only Arthur, the office boy, had witnessed his moment of glory.

***

He was inwardly ecstatic for the rest of the day and, unusually for him, Mr. Smith found himself constantly looking at the office clock in his keenness to leave.

At home that evening Mr. Smith restrained himself until he and his wife had finished their meal and she was washing the dishes. He was drying the cups and saucers when he chose the time to impart his great news. Mrs. Smith's reaction was what he had hoped for.

'If anyone deserves promotion, dear, it must be you. You work so hard carrying that office. I know he's gone now, and one shouldn't speak evil of the dead, but Mr. Matthews depended on you so much, didn't he? And as for that horrible Mr. Jardine, well, it's time he was put in his place.'

'That horrible Mr. Jardine' came back from his holiday the following Monday. After a brief interview with the Cost Accountant he

returned to the Section, making no comment about what had happened – just resuming his work at his usual desk as if everything was as it had been before he went away.

Mr. Smith was troubled. Had he won? Was it as simple as that? As the days passed he began to feel more relaxed, but he still felt uneasy. A response was inevitable, he knew his enemy too well to expect nothing in reply from him – but where was it and how would it show itself? The lack of reaction worried him. Was Jardine planning his counter-attack, or had he accepted that Harold was the winner? The fact that there was no obvious concern worried him. It simply didn't seem in character for the man he disliked so much.

With nothing said directly between the two men, Mr. Smith began to watch out for the internal post envelopes that came to him. He half expected an attack from his rival to come by this means. It was something he might have considered as a possibility had the situation been reversed, so why wouldn't Jardine? After all, to avoid speaking he had sent his neighbour memos through the system regularly since he'd started work here. But the brown envelopes that arrived twice a day didn't have the poisoned dart he expected.

Jardine continued to use his original desk, and the unused central desk showed a wider than ever rift between them. This added to Mr. Smith's unease. The two never made eye contact and as far as Mr. Smith was concerned Jardine seemed to be the perfect office colleague, hard working and conscientious – a man devoted to his work.

As time passed Mr. Smith found he was able to relax and feel confident that he really had won. Even so, his day now began by catching a different train each morning, one that put him at his desk thirty-five minutes earlier, and importantly, thirty-five minutes before his enemy. He knew his opponent was sneaky. It was too soon to lower his guard. He would savour the real enjoyment of his victory later.

***

'Just read that, both of you, then initial it and pass it to my secretary for filing.' It was four weeks after his promotion. The office was pleasantly warm, and Mr. Smith was startled from a near doze by the Cost Accountant's voice as he saw him handing a paper to his enemy. 'Well done...er, Sidney. Good thinking. We need more of that around the place.' He went back to his office without acknowledging Mr. Smith's presence.

Mr. Smith knew that he must force himself to look across at his colleague, and did so, to see him putting his initials to the paper with an untypical flourish. Then the single sheet was pushed over for him to read. It was similar to the mass of other inter-office documents that regularly circulated around the office. People who needed to see the paper were listed, and after reading it, each was expected to initial it and send it on to the next name.

The sequence of names on the list followed the rigorously enforced hierarchical system that existed in the Company of those days, one which put individuals in descending order of rank. Protocol insisted that people at the same level were listed in alphabetical order. There were about a dozen names on the list, starting, as always, with the Chief Accountant's.

Mr. Smith's eyes read down the list. There the names were, clear and indisputable.

'Jardine. S.J.'

The last name was his. The last name in the rankings of the office and the section.

‘Smith. H.’

The lack of a second initial had never hurt Mr. Smith more than it did at that moment. For a moment he hated his harmless, peace-loving father who was still alive and living quietly in Southport for not giving proper consideration to the choice of name for his first-born. Somehow he sensed that worse was to come. There was no reason to link this routine document with his enemy but, somehow he knew, that this was the moment he had been dreading. Uppermost in his mind was the fact that he was to behave at least as well as his foe had, and show no weakness or emotion, whatever happened.

Mr. Smith could sense, rather than see, that he was being watched by his neighbour as he forced himself to keep his hands from shaking, and to look down to read the single foolscap sheet. It was dated the previous day.

***

To. Mr. P.T. Raybould.

At yesterday's meeting of the Office Working Practices and Economies Committee, we discussed the suggestion that following a minor reorganisation in the Waste Recovery Section, certain items are surplus to requirements.

The Committee agreed with this view and decided that the Section Head's desk and the two telephones, internal and external, should be removed forthwith.

As there are now just two people employed in the Section, it was felt that they could easily use other telephones that are elsewhere in the Cost Office.

LAST ONE OFF THE TRAIN.

(Published in *Alfie's Dog*. February 2015).

Yes, it was definitely the same guy. Just last night he'd been the final fare of the shift and the last one of his week in the cab. It was a shift he hated but he had to do it – the boss insisted – and Ben was old fashioned enough to prefer working to being unemployed.

Another thing the boss insisted on was his drivers didn't call punters *'punters'*, anymore. Since he'd been away on that course they were now always *'clients'*. Whatever the lads in the cabs called 'em, unless the 'fares' tipped well that late shift was the worst of the week. That was unless he was working weekends, but then he'd have volunteered anyway. Ben remembered some of his punters – *sorry, Boss, clients* – and he wouldn't easily forget this particular bloke who was sitting just a foot or so away from him in Mike's usual seat in the main stand.

The cabbies normally remembered two sorts of passengers. Naturally enough the good tippers best of all – the generous types who might give them a note or two for the back pockets, not just the normal few bob. They all remembered the stingy, tight-fisted sort, and when they were sullen and grumpy as well, the news soon became shared knowledge with Ben and his mates. Ben certainly wouldn't easily forget this man. A drive in heavy rain all the way out to the posh new hotel on the ring road at half-one in the morning for a five-eighty fare and 'Keep the change, cabby' from six quid as if it was handing over a small fortune. And that was after lifting his case out of the boot, too.

That very same bloke was sitting next to him at the match. In one of the best seats in the ground and wearing the hated blue and white.

Sulky, mean, and he supported Athletic. A man, too, who had used a purse – something that Ben secretly despised. What a combination. The seat he was in was Mike's who'd had it for years. He sold his seat just for that day and had gone over to Bedford to his granddaughter's christening. 'Under duress' he had said, and the business nearly caused a family break-up. Mike had told Ben he'd been going and that his son 'had caved in to his missus and allowed her to choose today of all days for the sprog's christening. As a Town supporter he should have known better. You can see who wears the trousers there, can't you?'

He already knew this chap wasn't the sociable sort, making any sort of banter between the two unlikely. Ben was determined not to speak first. If anything, the man looked even less happy than he had last night. He seemed to be looking round for someone – anyone – sitting near him wearing the blue and white of Mallington Athletic and finding no-one, he spoke to Ben.

No 'Excuse me', no 'Hello' – nothing like that. No preamble – just straight in. Something or someone seemed to have upset him and he seemed even more surly than he had just a few hours ago in the early hours.

'I thought that youngster from Brazil was playing today. I don't see his name in the team. Is he injured or something? I've come a long way to see him playing here in Mallington. Especially today of all days in this particular match.'

Ben knew the man hadn't recognised him. A naturally polite man, Ben stayed calm.

'Oh, he's there alright. Here it is in the programme.' He pointed to the name on the page. 'Varian. In his usual place in mid-field. You must have looked in the wrong place, mate. You won't miss him when they start – he's a little cracker. It's only a question of how long we can keep him. They reckon Arsenal are trying to sign him.' The man looked again in his programme and said something.

Ben was a big man, and when he stood up he towered over his neighbour. 'I heard what you said then and I don't want more like it. Whatever your problem is, that sort of language won't solve anything. If you have a problem, keep it to yourself and don't try to involve everyone else in it. My daughter is sitting next to me and there are other women and kids nearby. No more of it – right? OK? Got that?' The man – much smaller and probably a bit older – looked cowed and nodded. He mumbled a grudging apology that Ben acknowledged. 'So, if you're willing to be reasonable, you can talk to me. Otherwise, don't waste your breath and my time.'

In the time left before kick-off, the story came out in a halting, subdued fashion. 'I'm a local man but this is my first visit to the town for years. Did alright over there in Brazil so now I live there. Supported Athletic since I was a kid and it's something you never lose. You probably know all about that with Town. I wanted to be here today, particularly at this game, as it's down to me that young Varian is playing. I paid his fare over and gave him an intro to the club chairman. I didn't know then if he was good enough to make the grade but I knew he was a decent player and very keen. The boy had written a couple of times that he was doing alright and playing in the reserves. Then another letter came saying he was in the first team. Obviously I was delighted and I've come over specially for today – the first time he will have turned out in the local derby. So that's it. I flew over and what do I find? The lad I'd recommended is playing for your lot. Naturally enough I assumed he'd followed up the lead I gave him into Athletic. I don't know what went wrong but I feel as if I've been kicked in the stomach by a horse. You must be a Mallington man so you'll know how the two clubs get on. They hate each other's guts.'

Ben didn't need telling about the level of rivalry in the town when it came to football. It went back generations to allegations of bribery involving a match referee and a result that meant that Town had been relegated and Athletic promoted. That was back in the early thirties. Nothing was ever proved but the legacy remained. *'Rivalry'* – a word not strong enough but it would do for starters. There were no neutrals in Mallington. You were born supporting one club or the other and your allegiances went down the generations. Ben decided to make a few non-committal, vaguely sympathetic noises and say nothing more. He simply let his mind go back a few months.

***

'Sir, I may not need your taxi, but I need somewhere to stay tonight here in Mallington. Not expensive, please. Can you help me?'

Ben had already sized up the questioner as he had come on to the station forecourt. His instant reaction to the haversack, plastic suitcase, cheap-looking clothes and general air of weariness from too many miles in a crowded train was a selfish one as he dismissed the hope of a big tip. His opinion strengthened when he saw that the potential passenger was little more than a boy. The graveyard shift was bad enough as it was, but a final run of the day with nothing extra in tips for him just about said it all. The evening was a write-off.

Certainly not English, probably foreign – that didn't worry him. He seemed a decent enough lad and polite with it.

'It's a bit late, young fella, and here in the town centre there's nowhere really cheap. Where are you from then?'

'From London Heathrow today, but I am from Brazil. I want to be somewhere near the football ground of Mallington Athletic F.C. I have come to England and hope to play for them. I have a letter of introduction to the Chairman of the Board of Directors − Mister Joseph Myers.'

'Look lad, just for tonight I'll take you home with me. Then we'll see. I won't rob you. My wife Renata Maria is Portuguese, so the language will suit you. She'll make you very welcome, talk the hind leg off you in your own lingo, feed you well and – as for the football, we can chat about that later. OK? I'm Ben Challiss by the way.'

'My name is Roberto Carlos Varian, Mr. Challis. Thank you very much. I have great pleasure in accepting your offer. What is the 'hind leg' meaning, please?'

The two drove off. Ben took the opportunity to tell Roberto all about Mallington's two Football League clubs. His views could easily be summarised in a few words. Mallington Athletic were rubbish, while Mallington Town was the team that any sensible, open-minded, true football-loving man should support. OK, to an outsider Athletic would seem to be a bigger and richer club from their lofty position in the league, but the real football fans, the ones who knew the game, recognised that Town's position a couple of places below their neighbour's was a false one and almost certainly just a temporary thing.

Ben managed to find a space to park the cab near his front door, took the boy in and after a moments' explanation he was instantly out of his depth. He had a smattering of his wife's language, but little more than that, and when she went off at ninety to the dozen he just gave up. She and the boy obviously hit it off. She went into the kitchen, Roberto following like a puppy dog and he came out some minutes later looking happy and at home.

'Your wife is so kind, Mr. Challis. And she cooks so well. I felt I was back in Sao Paolo.'

'Yes, Roberto. I am a lucky man. I expect you are ready for bed. I will show you your room and Renata will arrange breakfast before you go up. In the morning we will sort out this football business for you. Thank you for the letter you have given me to look at. I'll read it later.' The living-room door opened and a young woman came into the room. She looked enquiringly at Roberto who blushed and rose to his feet. 'This is Helena Josephine, our daughter. Like her mother, isn't she?'

Roberto stuttered over the introductions and couldn't take his eyes off the girl. Strikingly lovely, black shoulder length hair and a figure that would match any he had ever seen – he stood there slack-mouthed and smitten. Helena spoke a few words of Portuguese to the young man and in his embarrassment he struggled to respond sensibly. Ben sized up the situation and showed him upstairs to his bedroom.

When he came down again, the two women were talking and switched to English for his benefit. 'I think you have made a conquest there, Helena. The young man seems to fancy you. You won't fancy him though, when he goes for a trial with Athletic.'

'No I won't. Pity. He seems rather nice, actually, but for anyone who isn't a Town man I'm not interested.'

The resumption of the rapid-fire Portuguese left Ben out of his depth so he opened the letter he'd been given earlier.

It didn't give a positive introduction to Mallington Athletic and it was clear the writer had no direct contact to the club. This was from a longtime supporter of the club who currently lived abroad. It was a letter of hope – nothing stronger – the sort that any exiled supporter would write. He's used the Chairman's name, but it was obvious he didn't actually know him. Roberto had also told Ben that his well-wisher – Mr. Samuel Roberts – had given him some money for his journey from Brazil to England. It seemed just about enough to get him to the airport in Sao Paolo and not much further. Apparently the boy had used most of his savings on this gamble he had taken. Frankly the way Ben saw it was that the man seen by the boy as his benefactor had done him few favours – little beyond the least he could do with minimal trouble and outlay for himself.

Next morning he explained to Roberto that, out of season, the ground would be shut on a weekend, so nothing could be done till Monday. Common decency meant that he would help Roberto to where he wanted to go, but would not help him further. But, if he was prepared to consider the 'best team in Mallington' first, instead of 'that other lot', then he would be welcome to stay with the Challis family until things were sorted and he would be helped as much as possible to settle in.

That was under twelve months earlier. Roberto had made his choice, gone to Mallington Town and had a trial game. After an extended run in the junior side, then the second team, along with strict training and stamina building, he was now the bright young star of the first team, scoring goals regularly and being watched by the Premier League elite.

***

No, I won't tell this chap from Brazil what's happened over the last year. I won't tell him that a generous club gave me two season tickets to the best seats in the ground for what I'd done for them. Ben knew very well it wasn't all down to him. Without the young woman sitting next to him at every home game, Ben knew he'd still have been standing with his pals in his regular spot behind the Plympton Street goal. No, it was Helena really. On that first Sunday in the house the emphatic statement that she wouldn't be seen dead with an Athletic supporter or player – a remark of just general intent but one that had registered with the young Brazilian – that had done it.

***

The result was the right one for the home supporters. Mallington Town won 1- 0. It was special for three people in particular. Young Roberto had scored the winning goal and was a hero to half of the population of Mallington. To use a footballing term Helena was 'over the moon' and she and Roberto officially became engaged that evening. Happiest of all was Ben who had seen his team leapfrog their local rivals in the league table and had seen the man from Brazil skulk away before the final whistle without a backward look. The weekend wasn't so bad after all.

IT CAN BE ROUGH OUT THERE.

(Published in *Winamop.* February 2015)

There wasn't much left he believed in these days, but Adrian Dunnett raised his eyes and thanked his guardian angel – whoever or whatever he / she/ it was – every time he went through the door of *'Ben's Den.'* He recalled the moves he'd made, the stages that had taken him in just a few years from a grotty junk shop in a back-street in Salisbury, very like this dump, to his gallery in West London. The memories flooded back. Still, no need to be snooty about it, from different rungs of the ladder, both he and Ben were trying to do the same thing – sell stuff to the Great British Public and make a decent living out of it. And come to that, so was that Arab bloke from Harrods who just happened to have a bigger and posher shop than they had.

Once he'd had to do all of this to earn a crust: clocking up the miles in his old Volvo, praying he wouldn't be stopped and his tyres and brakes checked, scrabbling around looking for gear with a bit of profit left in it in all the antique shops, markets, fairs and sale rooms he could find, doing the knocking on doors bit, and then hoping he could find a customer in Joe Public, or even sometimes in desperation sell it on in the trade for more or less what he paid for it and glad to get rid.

As it came back to him, all he had to do was remind himself that he wasn't really working today; he was just out on the road on a semi-social basis. More or less a few days off. Well, sort of. Nowadays he had a handful of runners out doing all the leg work for him and working the long hours he used to do. So now: just switch off for a short break, let the posh bird he'd hired try to charm the punters – after all that's why he'd taken on Jocelyn, legs up to her armpits and Rodean voice – and as he'd told her 'I'm only a phone call away. But don't ring me unless it looks important.' Two or three days away from the shop, see a few people, look up a handful of old friends, then back to Kensington refreshed. That was the theory of it. And he might even pick up a bargain to pay his exes. Not that that was likely. Certainly not here amongst all this tat.

'Hi Ben. How tricks?'

'Oh, hello Ade. Long time no see. Not good. Trade's like the dodo actually.'

'Family OK?'

'Maggie's expecting again.'

'You should be locked up. Five kids and another coming. As I've said before – have the snip.' The two talked for a while, then Adrian walked into the small storeroom at the rear. Ben followed him. 'What d'ye reckon to this then? Nice isn't it?'

He passed Adrian a small, framed oil painting. It showed a two-masted sailing ship battling against a severe storm. He walked over to the window, struggling to find better light though the unwashed glass and grubby curtain.

'It's still wet where you've signed it, Ben, and you're a bigger fool than I thought you were. It's a pretty little picture – or it was. What did you give for it – a fiver?' Ben looked sheepish. 'Fifteen quid, actually. Some old girl from Poole wandered in with a few bits in a Tesco bag. I bought some jewellery from her as well. Nothing special, but there's got to be something left in it for me.'

'And you felt sorry for her. My God. Somebody saw you coming alright. At five I'd have given you a profit on it, but now you've killed it stone dead. And the name you signed it with – George R. Midleton? At least you've managed to spell it right with just one d. Do you know just how stupid you really are? What do you know about the artist's name you picked? Tell me, honestly, what do you know about him?'

Ben went to his desk. On top was an opened hard-backed book with illustrations – some in black and white, some in colour. 'There' he said triumphantly. 'All his info – a bio, dates, where he exhibited, which galleries he'd been shown in, everything. That's in *Pullen.* You can't argue with that. Standard reference work and all that. There you are: *George R. Midleton. Marine Artist. 1820 – 1882.* Right there in front of you, Ade – in black and white. You can't argue with that, now, can you?'

An unchastened Adrian responded. 'What are you now, Ben? Twenty-four, twenty-five? Over the years you haven't got any brighter, have you? Yes, you're right, of course. Pullen's *'Listing of British Maritime Artists'* is the Bible in its field. No argument. A fine work. Everybody refers to it.' He picked up Ben's copy and looked at the cover.

'In all your little library over there do you have a later copy? They do Year Book updates, you know. Annually.' He couldn't keep the sarcasm out of his voice. The older man walked over to Ben's collection of reference books, a collection similar to that he could find in hundreds of premises like this all over the country. There they were - the inevitable *Millers Guide* and *Lyles*, old copies of the *Antiques Trade Gazette* in untidy piles, price guides, auction house catalogues. 'Nothing newer than 5 years old here, old boy. Your copy of *Pullen* is 7 years out of date. No good at all unless it's current.'

‘But the basic info. That doesn’t change does it? What’s your point, then?’

‘My point, Ben, is this. You know how prolific Peter Pullen is with his writing. You’ve seen how many books he’s written, and how highly regarded he is by anyone who knows anything about art. But have you met Peter Pullen? Well, I have and I know Peter very well. He’s a lovely guy with a savage sense of humour. Well, for years now in the trade we’ve known that his listings are heaven-sent for cowboys – and we both know how many there are of those about: don’t we, Ben? These characters just find a painting, let’s say for instance, a sailing ship at sea in a storm – I’m just picking a thought at random you understand, of course – then they look at the list of names of marine artists who might have painted a picture like it, then slap on the name. They don’t try to copy a signature – just the name is enough for them. The Auctioneer’s work-experience trainee or tea-boy, or somebody on minimum wage, checks in the reference book, sees the name and it goes up for sale. Then some innocent member of Joe Public buys it on the strength of a sale-house catalogue. Sounds familiar, does it, old boy?’

‘Peter wasn’t happy about this – you can’t blame him, can you? – so he decided to get his own back. He didn’t overdo it, but in several of his listings he inserted a name – let’s say *‘An artist who never was.’* With year-books you can do that easily and regularly. Peter didn’t tell a soul, not even his editor. He just went ahead and did it, and the Year Books as they came out started to include these invented names and bios. Then one day he was visiting his folks in the Cotswolds and popped into the local sale-room. And you can guess what he found. That’s right; a painting with the signature of an artist who had never existed – just one of Peter’s *‘Dream Team’* as he’d started to call them.

Of course as soon as he'd seen what had happened he withdrew the name from the following year's new updated edition.'

'Nice little story, eh Ben? I hope it makes you think before you get out your paint-set another time.'

Ben by now was looking extremely solemn. He could see the fifteen pounds he'd spent going down the drain. Trade was ropey and the six-monthly shop rent bill was due next week. Maggie was edgy enough already about the baby so he was in for a rough time at home.

'You might well look concerned, young Benjamin. There's more to come. Some people claim not to believe in coincidence, but me, personally, I do. And so should you. The forged name that Peter Pullen happened to see that day in Broadway was – you've got it – George R. Midleton, the very name you've picked. The police were called in and they're still looking for the con-man. And if they find this little effort of yours they're going to believe the earlier one was yours too – and who could blame them?'

'So, dear boy, as well as telling you to keep your head down let me give you some advice. One, there are lots and lots of very nice, very honest people in this business – but there are some out and out rogues. Be careful what you do and who you do business with in future.'

'Two. If you're using reference books, make sure you use a current edition. I know they're not cheap but it isn't something to skimp on, even when times are hard.'

'So, thanks for the coffee and I'll see you around. Try not to get too low, there's always a silver lining. Love to Maggie and the kids.' He turned to go. Ben put his hand up to delay him.

‘Ade. I’m bothered about that picture. I know you know about these things. Far more than I do. Would it be any use to you? You could have it for what I paid for it.’

‘Sorry Ben, but there’s no way I could go to fifteen for it. I’d like to help – but....’

‘Can’t you get the signature off again? It’s a nice little painting otherwise.’

‘Yes, I can see that but removing what you’ve added – it’s not something I can do. Sorry.....But I’ll tell you what. Let me have it for five and I’ll take a chance. At least that way it would never be linked with you if the police got involved.’

***

Two days later Adrian was back in his flat after his few days on the road. He looked again at the little seascape and saw the cryptic swirl in the bluey-green of the heaving waters. Yes, there it was just as he’d recognised in the little shop – the disguised monogram JRE, which an experienced eye could see and which the current edition of *Pullen* confirmed as the mark of John Russell Edwards, one of the Britain’s greatest maritime painters.

He smiled as he remembered telling Ben that removing the forged signature was something he couldn’t do. That was true enough – but he knew a man who could.

No: he hadn’t lied. He thought back to the time in the Boscombe shop. What he’d done in essence was give a young dealer some help and advice in his chosen line of work. Tuition, coaching, consultancy, whatever you called it, a fee was not unreasonable to expect for a service like that, was it? As for the profit he’d make on the little oil – it would be massive but he wouldn’t be greedy. Ben did have money problems so he'd send off a cheque for maybe a hundred or two. Send it to Maggie personally; she'd always had more sense than her husband would ever have. After all, everyone expects a bloke to look after his kid brother, don't they? Being family and all that.

THE SAME – BUT DIFFERENT.

(Published in *Winamop*. October 2012).

I had a phone call one evening from a guy called Kevin. Kevin Trotter to be exact. I didn't know him and the call came right out of the blue. All because my name is David Cornwell and I live in a little village in Dorset called Winsome. Not clear? Well let me explain.

I'm a writer. Like two very well-known authors, Patricia and Bernard who share my surname. Bernard writes the *Sharpe* military stories and Patricia – American forensic stuff. I like what Bernard writes, and though I haven't read any of Patricia Cornwell's books, my wife rates them highly and I know what else she reads, so they won't be rubbish. As for me – you'll never have heard of me – nor what I write. I'm a part-time writer of short stories – right at the other end of the literary greasy pole.

But last month I had a story published – my fourth one actually, a tally that's something I'm secretly rather proud of, and this Kevin bloke had seen it. What he'd read was *'Hidden waters'* in the winter edition of *The Reading Room.* Now, that's one of the mags that shows where the author comes from, so I was listed as David Cornwell of Winsome, Dorset. Cute name, Winsome, isn't it? That's my little joke. Original, too. Good, isn't it? With a full name and a home village shown, it was easy enough to find me in the 'phone book.

Kevin, apparently, is a committee member of the *Inky Fingers Club* which, he told me, is a group of wannabe writers and scribblers in and around Chulmington – that's about fifteen miles away. He's new to the area, has just been voted on to the committee as Events Organiser, and is obviously very keen to make his mark. Reading between the lines from my own experiences of numerous committees, if a new member arrives on the scene and seems just half-way keen, he'll be co-opted on PDQ and given plenty of things to do. I've seen it a few times before and it's happened to me on occasions too. That is until I learned better and began to know the ropes. In many committees, so often it's the same few people who seem to finish up doing most of the work. So, if some work can be farmed out and passed on to a willing mug – sorry, volunteer – well, you jump at the chance. Delegation they call it. I've heard it called other things as well – a bit less flattering.

Back to my tale. This Kevin bloke said how much he'd liked my story and put it to me that he'd like me to talk about my work – as a published writer – at one of the Society meetings. Of course I was flattered, who wouldn't be? I stood there with the phone to my ear preening myself. Then, with provisional agreement between us about that, he suddenly changed tack, and started talking about John le Carré.

Now this is where this Kevin bloke put two and two together, but clearly, he's no mathematician because he made it five. He told me that he's a long-term admirer of John le Carré's writing, and knowing two things about him – that his real name is David Cornwell and that he lives somewhere in the South West – well, he jumped in feet first. He had come to the conclusion that I was J le C, and that I was having a bit of a busman's holiday with a switch of style and genre from my usual writing by turning out the short story that he'd just read. Being a literary man Kevin couldn't resist using the word 'hedonistic.' And he assumed that J le C had put it out under his real name too, believing that no-one would make the connection. That is unless you were as keen-eyed and observant as Kevin Trotter believed he was. To be honest, when I think about it, apart from the coincidence of the names, it would have been difficult to think of a plot further removed from anything that John le C had written – and I've read most, if not everything, he's had published. My little effort was a thing that you would class as sci-fi, with a time traveller from earth managing to avert a war between two alien peoples. Not quite George Smiley and The Circus territory, is it?

Then, when he went on with telling me about who he thought I really was, it was clearly a complete mix-up and misunderstanding. Obviously, I tried to put him right. The trouble was, he wouldn't believe me. He was convinced it was a matter of undue modesty and a 'big name' trying to retain a degree of privacy. But Kevin had a theory – and he'd made up his mind: so he didn't want anything as inconvenient as a fact getting in the way.

He kept on and on about how keen the folks down there were, and what an appreciative audience he would guarantee for my talk. Anywhere between fifteen and twenty, he said, in *'a pleasant upstairs room in a nice pub'*. Real Ale too, he said, but as a wine man, that meant nothing to me. After listening to all his spiel about his John le C idea, I told him that I'd decided not to talk to his members after all, and finally got off the phone thinking that was the end of it. No way. He'd already wheedled my email address out of me, and messages from him started to arrive regularly. Eventually he wore me down. I sent him a reply and said I would go and speak to his members on the clear understanding that I was David Cornwell – a nobody – and not John le Carré. He agreed, we fixed a date, and that was that.

***

Came the day and it turned out rather well. I kicked off by making it clear to everyone just who I wasn't. Kevin had taken charge of me when I arrived, and when I told them this he did get a few rather dirty looks. Obviously, despite what I'd agreed with him, it looked as if he'd persisted in spinning this line and a handful of folks had fallen for it. Come re-election time for the club committee he may pay for that. Even so, the evening was decent enough.

Over the years I've had quite a lot of experience talking to groups of people as part of my job – anything from half-a-dozen people up to several hundred. Once I had to try to quieten a screaming mob of angry women – that was back in the days when I was trying to run a factory and stop a strike. But that's another story. So there was no problem there to bother me, and I just talked about my own efforts trying to get a story published, the mass of rejections and the occasional *'Yes, please, we like it'* from an editor. I told them where to look in *Duotrope* for outlets for anything they'd written, and stressed how important I had found it was to put a story away and return to it with a fresh eye after a decent break. And other tips – formatting, attention to proof-reading and so on – I was happy to pass on. All the little things I'd learned the hard way. There were some excellent questions at the end too before we all adjourned downstairs to the bar.

I got the usual vote of thanks at the end and I came away happy enough, even after turning down the offer of a few quid for my exes. End of story I thought. Not so. Just days later I had a phone call from a chap who had been at the meeting. He was from another society over in Exeter and he wanted me to speak to them sometime on a similar theme. I was quite flattered and this time I didn't hesitate – but this time said I needed something for my petrol money.

***

The big surprise came about a week after that in the form of an email from John le Carré himself. The real McCoy, this time. What he said was that he'd heard though a contact about the meeting over at

Chulmington. Once he'd accepted that there were no intentions to dupe anyone, and that we really did have the same name, he was quite happy – and amused by the whole business of the mix-up.

He said he'd heard good things about the talk and, would you believe it? – What he'd heard had triggered an idea. Would I mind if he wrote a short story using this idea? Wow! THE John le Carré asking MY permission to allow him to write a story about ME? Unbelievable.

I sent him a reply back pronto. And did I agree? You bet I did. Wouldn't you have? Of course you would. Alright, the email was dated April 1, and as for the email address he used, well, we all know how easy it is to give yourself a new identity anytime with Hotmail, but what clinched it for me was this simple fact. Who ever heard of anyone making up a story from such a feeble little nothing? Only a proper writer like John le Carré would be good enough to do that. So it must have been him, mustn't it?

THE TWO SEATS.

(Published in *Fiction on the web*. June 2017).

The man walked through the door of The Red Lion and hesitated. Faced with a choice of two doors, after a moment's consideration he went through the one to his right, which had Snug in ornate gilt letters on its glazed upper section. At the bar he ordered a half pint of local bitter, sipped it approvingly, and turned round to face the room. As his eyes wandered around his face changed from uncertainty to take on a look of growing contentment.

In the corner to his left next to a stone fireplace, which had an unlit log fire, there was a large, cushioned wooden chair with arms. Oak and clearly old it looked inviting. The man went across to the chair and sat down.

'You can't sit there. Sorry. It's spoken for. That's Old Seth's seat'.

The stranger looked up. He had thought he was alone in the room. It was early in the evening, and a Tuesday anyway, normally a quiet time for a pub, but he could see now that there was someone else after all.

The second man spoke again from his bench seat in a corner. 'He'll be in later. He's usually pretty punctual'.

The newcomer stood up. 'I'll sit here then'.

He made to move to an identical seat on the opposite side of the fireplace.

'Sorry lad, you're out of luck. That one's reserved as well. It's Old Jack's seat. You'd better come and sit next to me. You'll be alright here. The name's Summers – Fred Summers'.

‘Thank you’.

The man moved over and sat down.

‘My name’s Jenkins’.

The two men shook hands. Fred spoke.

‘You’re not from round here are you? That twang isn’t local. Where are you from then – London?’

The Snug began to fill up as the conversation continued. Mr. Jenkins was from Margate and had come up to Derbyshire to spend a short time with his son. That young man lived in the new development to the east of Moorsedge and commuted to Sheffield. Mr. Jenkins had tried ‘the yuppy pub’ on the estate and didn’t like it. However, he did like ‘the occasional beer’ so here he was.

The two new acquaintances clearly both liked to chat. Each found the other’s company increasingly congenial as they discovered they had much in common. They were both retired civil servants, both widowers, both keen on sport, and increasingly disillusioned with the way the world was going. The pub filled steadily and Mr. Jenkins, a man experienced in the ways of public houses, could see why. The atmosphere was pleasant and relaxed, the landlord was a jovial man who appeared to enjoy a good tale and seemed to have a fund of jokes to draw on; and as the two men agreed ‘George there knows his beer and serves a good pint’. The two had gravitated to pints by then.

Obviously most of the regular drinkers there were from the village and this was their local. Naturally Fred knew them all and seemed utterly relaxed in this setting. One table had a small group of men who, Mr. Jenkins thought out loud to his companion, ‘probably walked over from the estate where my boy is. It’s a help when you don’t need a car. You can have that extra drink and feel safe about it’. As this was early in the week, he could imagine how busy it would be on a Friday or Saturday.

Almost all the seats in the Snug were taken, but the two near the fireplace remained empty. Fred explained that it was a little local custom and that the seats were reserved for the village's oldest beer-drinking inhabitants.

Then – 'That's Old Seth just coming in'.

Seth collected his pint and took his seat.

'Eighty-seven'.

Mr. Jenkins felt he must have asked the question without realising it.

Minutes later – 'And that's Old Jack' – as they watched him sit down opposite.

'A mere boy. He's only eighty-six. Just watch this and listen'.

The old men faced each other. There was nothing to mark them out from other old men. They had white hair – plenty of it in Seth's case, less in Jack's, while Seth used a stick and Jack didn't. They were dressed normally enough, each of them in darkish suits that were shiny with wear, with white mufflers around their necks. They both had caps that they took off when they sat. As Seth had gone to his seat Mr. Jenkins couldn't avoid hearing his boots – black, highly polished and very squeaky. Each sipped his pint. Neither spoke for several minutes.

Mr. Jenkins began to speak.

'But what...?' only to be cut short by his companion. 'Just hang on a minute'.

Old Jack spoke first - just one word.

'Larwood'.

The response was snapped out by Old Seth almost before Jack had finished.

'Tyson. Easy. Yards faster. No contest. Stick to what you know about if there is owt'.

There was a mumble from Old Jack that could have been 'Silly old fool. Everybody knows it's Larwood'.

The two old men glared at each other in silence for minutes on end.

Then 'Tyson' – issued as a single word challenge.

'What on earth is going on? It's just two silly old men in their cups. Yet surely they can't be drunk at this time in the evening. Are they all there?'

'Just hang on. I'll get another drink in before we go. Pint is it? I'll save the story till tomorrow – it'll keep – that is if you can make it then. If you're free in the morning meet me at the bowling-green across the road at 10.30. After all, we're both men of leisure, aren't we? How does that suit you?'

The arrangement suited Mr. Jenkins very well. He left The Red Lion minutes after Old Jack and Old Seth did. They left separately without having said another word to each other. The only words they spoke were to thank Fred Summers as he bought each of them a drink.

***

Next morning was beautiful late summer weather, ending an exceptionally dry season. The bowling green was obviously regularly watered and showed no signs of the drought. The single green was in superb order. Fred was already there when Mr. Jenkins arrived. He was sitting in a seat at one corner of the green. There was another seat at the next corner on the same side. Both were placed to catch as much sun as possible.

Mr. Jenkins went to join him. Fred unscrewed a flask and poured out two cups of coffee. He added something from a small hip-flask. They both sipped appreciatively.

'I'm just admiring the condition of this lot. You know, the groundsman runs the local Post Office and does all this in his own time. Fifty quid a year is his honorarium, as they call it – and it's worth every penny. What we'd ever do if he left the village I don't know'.

'I see you're curious about the green. It's the local game – crown green bowls with the middle of the green built up higher than the edges. Much more skill to it than the flat grass you play on down south, or so we always think. You have to compensate for much more this way when you bowl. The waywardness of the green as well as the bias from the bowls. It's a fine game. Quite a challenge. Needs some skill to be any good at it. We'll have a game or two before you go back'.

'They'll be here soon, so I'll tell the tale before they arrive. Then perhaps we can go and have a pint later. That'll be alright, then?' Mr. Jenkins was beginning to enjoy his little holiday.

***

'Well, it's like this. I got most of the early part from my father; he's gone now, God bless him; but he was a local man born and bred, just as Jack and Seth are, and they all grew up as lads together. It seems that as young men both of them were very keen on sport – mad keen. That's true of many young chaps, of course, but with them it was exceptionally so. Not only were they very keen, but they were both pretty good at cricket and football. The village had teams for both games - we still have – but Seth and Jack were a lot better than the village sides were, so they joined outside clubs in higher standard leagues. Incidentally, they both had a trial with the County but neither of them was signed up. Derbyshire had some fine bowlers in those days, so you really had to be good to make it. I know you like your cricket so you might remember – Cliff Gladwin, Les Jackson, men like that. Players who got their England caps in time'.

'Anyway, each of them thought he was the best for miles around, so every time they met in a game the gauntlet was really thrown down. There was a sort of 'Cock o' the Walk' feel about it'.

'At the age they were they had their eyes on girls, of course, as well as the sport, but unfortunately they both fancied the same girl in the village. She went off with somebody else eventually, but that's not really part of the story. Add this rivalry over a girl to competition on the sports field, and you have a recipe for trouble'.

'Anyway, the way Dad told it to me, one cricket season the two found themselves on opposite sides in a key match. One of the two neutral umpires that the league had selected hadn't arrived, so the captains and the other umpire agreed to allow a member of the batting side to be the second umpire. This second man would stand at square leg every over, so he would only have to rule on stumpings or runs out with the 'proper' umpire making most of the major decisions; caught, lbw – things like that'.

'Fairly straight forward you would think, and it's a normal enough practice in cricket at its lower levels. Happening all the time'.

'Anyroad, Jack's side batted first and made a decent score in what was always going to be a close match. Jack himself was out first ball so he wasn't in a good mood - and that's putting it mildly. Seth's team started to bat and their captain was in and making a good few and looking good for more. Jack came on to bowl and was being thrashed all round the field – that's what Seth says anyway – then, Jack says – he bowled a beauty and the other team's captain was stumped; out of his ground by a yard or more'.

'Unfortunately for Jack, Seth was umpiring at square leg and gave the batsman 'not out'. Seth says he didn't have a good view because a fielder was in his way, so they gave the batsman the benefit of the doubt. Personally I don't see why the benefit shouldn't go to the bowler some of the time – but that's for another time. So, Seth's team went on to win the match by a handful of runs. Dad says they nearly came to blows about it on the field, and later on after the match'.

'Obviously, Jack wanted revenge. His opportunity came during the following football season. It happened because the side Seth played for had a match against another team (not Jack's). He was a spectator that time, and being known to most of the players on the field, was asked to deputise when one of the linesmen twisted his ankle or something'.

'Jack waited until Seth was going through with an almost certain goal in front of him, then flagged him up for offside. Of course, the Referee could do nothing about it. He had to take his linesman's word for it so he whistled when he saw the flag go up'.

'They were each in their twenties then, and they're both well turned eighty now, so that's been the length of their feud. They've never lived anywhere else except here in the village, just a few doors away from each other, and they haven't spoken a civil word to each other in all those years'.

Mr. Jenkins had been enjoying the sunshine, sipping his drink and listening intently to all this.

'The story's interesting enough up to there,' he said, 'but what's all this 'Larwood and Tyson' business about then?'

'Well,' said Fred, putting down the flask from which he had just poured refills for them both, 'they're too old now to fight out their feud on a pitch so they fight about sport in a different way'.

'For instance, 'Larwood and Tyson'. You know who they are, of course? Harold Larwood was the fast bowler in the 'Bodyline' Test Series while Frank Tyson and Brian Statham bowled the Aussies out the '54/'55 Tour. The point is they were both exceptionally fast, and who was the faster is a matter that really never can be settled. In other words, it's a matter where Seth's opinion is as good as Jack's and visa versa, and there's no way whatsoever they or anybody else can say which one is right, and which one is wrong'.

'Every now and then one of 'em will try to think up a reason for backing their man - some vaguely recalled incident or something they've read. Neither of them is going to win, but they keep trying. The silliest thing about it is, I don't know about Larwood, he was before their time, but I know for a fact that neither of them ever saw Frank Tyson bowl'.

'If they're not arguing about those two, then it's about Stanley Matthews and Tom Finney. Again, who can ever say who was the better of those two, eh? I certainly can't and I saw them both play quite a few times. Different, certainly – but one better than the other? No-one can say. These two old chaps never did see them play to my knowledge'.

'Then there's United and Wednesday, County and Forest. They'll use anything to try to win an argument. There might be something in one of the newspapers, and we all know what rubbish they'll print to sell a few copies. Really, it's a form of jousting by proxy'.

'The daftest thing of all, though, is when they argue about tennis. Nowadays there is a court in Moorsedge – it's down there near the Village Hall. It gets a lot of use around Wimbledon time, but otherwise it's just the club members who give it any usage. Round here, tennis used to be regarded as a bit of a posh game and for girls and sissies. Working class people wouldn't dream of playing the game back then; certainly that would have been the case when Jack and Seth were young men. I very doubt if either of them has ever held a tennis racket in his life, yet you should hear them go on about Borg and McEnroe. I sometimes despair and think they're barmy, I really do. They've lost it. No, they haven't of course, it just seems like it'.

'No – that's not fair. They're a pair of decent enough old men really. They live in the past as I suppose most old people so, anyway. Just as we probably will when our turn comes'.

'It's a bit like you and me – both cricket lovers, both supporting different counties. Two counties that each has a top flight wicket-keeper. Bob Taylor from up here and Alan Knott from down in Kent, your county. I reckon our man's better – but I expect you have a different point of view. We could argue about that till Kingdom Come and never settle it'.

'Both the old men lost their wives some years back – about the same time as it happened – so there's no-one at home for them to annoy. Here's one of them now'.

Mr. Jenkins recognised Old Seth from his stick and squeaky boots.

'They sit here most of the day, you know. It doesn't matter whether anyone's actually playing or not, so long as it stays fine'.

Old Jack appeared a few minutes later and sat down. It was on the same bench as Seth, but at the opposite end of a seat made for four or five. There was nothing resembling a greeting.

'Let's go across and I'll introduce you'.

As they reached the seat, Seth was gloating over United's current good form. Jack didn't have a response ready. He looked a bit sheepish and said nothing.

'Morning, Seth. Morning, Jack. Both alright then, are we? Did you notice this chap with me in the pub last night? It's Mr. Jenkins. He's staying with his son over at the new estate for a few days. He's from Margate'.

Seth was the first to speak.

'Howdo, lad. Margate – that's down south, isn't it?'

Jack chimed in. 'Essex or Surrey or somewhere'.

'Do you play?' Jack motioned to the bowling green.

'Flat greens down there, aren't they? With a little white jack. No proper game for a man, that. Looks easy enough – child's play really'.

Seth thought he saw his opportunity.

'You're a youngish chap, aren't you?' (At sixty-four Mr. Jenkins was flattered). 'Did you ever see Frank Tyson bowl?'

Instantly Jack responded. 'Take no notice of the old fool. What do you reckon to Tom Finney, eh? The best ever, wasn't he?'

Fred nudged Mr. Jenkins. 'They won't miss us, you know. Once we've gone they'll lose patience with the argument and go home, or doze off in the sun. This morning has already used up their talk ration for two or three days. They probably won't speak to each other again till Friday and then they'll only argue'.

Mr. Jenkins and Fred left the pair and had a drink and a sandwich in The Red Lion. As Mr. Jenkins was due to return home early the following day he didn't have the chance to study Jack and Seth further on his visit.

***

It was April the following year when Robin Jenkins invited his father up to stay again. On the day of his arrival Mr. Jenkins went to his 'favourite local hostelry', entered the Snug as he had done months previously, and sat where he had then. He was the first of the evening's customers. Fred Summers arrived and joined him. Fred seemed subdued.

'They buried Old Seth last week. He fell downstairs one morning. No chance at all at his age. Broke his neck'.

He took a generous gulp of his drink.

'I went round to tell Old Jack when I heard. I always tried to keep an eye on them both if I could – because of Dad I suppose. Jack never batted an eyelid. All he could say was 'Silly old bugger. Couldn't he see where he was going?'

'I offered to take him along to the funeral but he didn't seem to want to know about it. He just went up to the bowling green and sat in his usual seat'.

'In the pub here we had a whip-round and sent a big wreath, and any of us who could go went to the Church for the funeral. There was nobody in Seth's family who would need money after he went, so anything that was left from the collection we gave to the Vicar's

Charities Fund. We all felt – here in the pub that was – that as a mark of respect to Old Seth we'd keep his seat empty for the time being'.

'A nice gesture'. That was Mr. Jenkins.

Fred went silent again.

'The night of the funeral Old Jack came in as usual. He didn't have to put his hand in his pocket once that night. Everyone felt it was somehow a bit special, and all his drinks were bought for him. Actually, though, he never did have a lot to drink, did Old Jack. He sat there all evening in his normal seat. He spoke if anyone spoke to him but that was all'.

'I saw him once or twice looking at Seth's old seat but never once did he refer to him. I noticed he left the pub a bit earlier than usual that night'.

'He didn't come here the following evening, and when I didn't see him at the bowling green the day after that, I went round to his cottage on Old Mill Lane. When I knocked there was no reply so I let myself in. Jack was one of that generation that never locked its doors – he always said it wasn't necessary. Haven't times changed, eh?'

'The door from the street opens straight into the living room of these old cottages, of course, but he wasn't there, and he didn't reply when I called. I went upstairs and found him in that tiny front bedroom of his'.

'I was shocked when I saw him. He'd become an old, old man. Of course, he was that anyway, but somehow he never quite seemed it before then. Almost as if he'd put years on in just a couple of days'.

'He was cold even under his heavy blanket. He'd obviously been sweating a lot, and had wet himself, and was rambling away about something. I called the Doctor and she was there quite quickly. Jack

Would you please advise the people concerned, and pass on to Mr. Sidney Jardine of the Waste Recovery Section the Committee's appreciation of his suggestion.

As you know, the Company is always keen to encourage suggestions that show how deeply employees at all levels take an interest in their work. Mr. Jardine's understanding of the value of cost-effective communications and utilisation of resources is to be highly commended.

The usual Cash Award will be sent to Mr. Jardine in due course.

Signed. J. R. Jones. Chief Personnel Officer.

Mr. Smith kept his eyes on the paper for a minute or so after he finished reading it. He knew he had to look up, but dreaded the gloating and triumph that he would see from his neighbour. He forced himself to look to his side, and saw his enemy, clearly waiting for their eyes to meet.

Young Arthur was the only other witness to this moment. He insisted that he saw Mr. Jardine look at his colleague and wink with his left eye. No-one believed him though. Arthur was known for inventing little tales and this was just too unlikely to be true.

didn't approve of women doctors – at least not for men – but she was splendid. In no time she had the ambulance round, and they took him off to hospital. I went along with him, of course. He died in the night. That was last night. I wasn't with him when he went'.

'So that's the last of those two. A generation gone within a few days. That's the way it is'.

'I have a bit of a theory. It's not rocket science or anything – fairly obvious really, but I reckon that Jack and Old Seth had a sort of marriage. Probably they had shared as many experiences together in the seventy to eighty years since they grew up together as most men do with their wives. So, when Old Seth went it left Jack with nothing to live for. It left him nothing else to do but die. Is that a bit too far-fetched you reckon?'

Mr. Jenkins didn't think it was and said so. The two men drank a toast to the two empty seats.

They were both in a sombre mood so Mr. Jenkins decided to pass on his news in an attempt to lighten the atmosphere. His son, Robin, had suggested that his father came to live with him after moving up from Margate. This would give Mr. Jenkins constant contact with his six year-old grandson and he had jumped at the chance.

Naturally it couldn't happen overnight – there was a house to sell as well as other details to finalise – but give it time and The Red Lion would have another regular.

Fred didn't react in the way that Mr. Jenkins had hoped.

'Sorry, lad. My mind's on other things at the moment. Old Jack had no relatives left that I know of, so arranging the funeral details is down to me'.

Mr. Jenkins left him to his thoughts as he went across to the bar to order two more beers. Fred had a question to go with the unsettled, slightly wistful look on his face as they re-settled themselves.

'Would you say you were a conservative man, with a small 'c' that is? I mean, do you believe in the continuation of local traditions and that not everything that is old is bad, and certainly not that anything new has to be better? And that change shouldn't automatically wipe out what's been before?'

Mr. Jenkins nodded but didn't speak.

'Well then, seeing that you're going to be a regular here in our local, how about you and me filling those two empty seats by the fire. In due course, eh? Give it a bit of time for respect's sake, and then move over?'

Mr. Jenkins nodded his head and stuck out his hand in agreement.

'Yes? Take that as settled, shall we? Remember, we're trying to keep a local tradition going'.

The two men sat in silence, sipping their drinks. Then Fred spoke. There was a challenging note in his voice as he looked Mr. Jenkins in the eye.

'Now the on this matter of old traditions. I think we should try to do it properly – do the right thing. I reckon that fellow of yours, Alan Knott, is a good enough wicketkeeper but our man's better. He didn't bat as well so they didn't pick him for England. Even a Kent man has to agree with that. Am I right?'

Mr. Jenkins' concern at where the conversation was leading must have been more obvious than he thought.

Fred looked across and winked. 'Don't worry, lad. I'm only joking – right now that is. Perhaps in the future – who knows? Custom, practice and old traditions, eh? When is it you expect to come up this way?'

'Let's have another drink, shall we? My shout'.

FOR EVERY WINNER THERE'S A LOSER.

(Published in *Winamop.* December 2012).

Inside his head Rodney didn't try to pretend about his writing. He knew his limitations, and finding plots for his short stories was something he wasn't good at – his own original ideas that was, and not just a variation on something he'd seen or read somewhere else. No matter how hard he tried, whatever he worked on, somehow it finished up never far away from someone else's concept.

Not this time though. OK, so this new idea was prompted by that thing on ITV a few weeks back, but his jump from that plot – a bit routine he'd thought at the time – to this guy contemplating killing his wife after a massive win was miles away from what he'd watched. A winning lottery ticket was about the only thing they had in common. This time he had a sure-fire winner, and he knew it.

Something that might shut 'em up down in the Claims Department where he'd resigned himself to the comments that were regularly thrown at him.

'Rodney. Will you write longer stories when you get better, then?'

'Are you going to make as much money as that Rowlings woman?'

'So, you write the short stuff to practice for writing proper books, do you Rod?'

'Proper books' – the term always wound him up but he did his best just to ignore it. He knew his day would come. Like Del Boy used to say – *'This time next year, Rodney.....'*

Then he became *'a published author.'*

The acceptance of *'The early bird'* – just one story out of nineteen submitted to various editors – had come right out of the blue.

When he saw his story in *Charisma* – after the initial glow of pride – he felt disappointed and deflated. Some of his precise formatting had been ignored, and the closing paragraph that included the all-important twist in the tale was missing. Nobody reading his little masterpiece would ever have known that the vicar's wife had been involved in the thefts all along.

To a man who tried so hard to do a solid job on his proof-reading the results were sloppy and nothing like the copy he had sent in. And they even got his name wrong. There it was, up there in bold type – *Wilkins* instead of *Wilkinson.*

The rest of the little A5 magazine didn't impress him and the stories were a poor lot. Rod regretted signing up as and paying his ten quid subscription, so when *Charisma* folded soon afterwards he wasn't surprised. He e-mailed the editor ('ex-editor by now' as he was very keen to stress to Rod), but the promised refund cheque still hadn't arrived.

So with his Great Idea burning away in his head, Rod settled down for the evening at his laptop. As usual, Mary was downstairs in front of the massive Sony HD set, chocolates already opened, and impatient for *Coronation Street* to start. *Frost* was to follow and apart from the loo and a cup of tea, Mary wouldn't move much from her favourite seat. 'She might lose a few pounds if she did move more.' He found he was thinking things like that rather a lot these days.

Rod's stories weren't finished quickly. What took the time before he pressed a single key was his painstaking reading-up and preparation – his 'homework.'

His own reading for pleasure had given him a massive respect for the top writers in the Spy / Thriller genre – people like Frederick Forsythe and John le Carré. Research, detail, background – these big boys knew how to do it. So, read, watch and learn, Rod. Study the subject, make notes, and thank the Lord for search engines. His desk-pad had a few jottings on it.

'Man, married twenty something years, unhappy marriage – his wife has let herself go. Winning ticket – massive win on lottery. Decides to start afresh – kill wife and take up with young girl in the office.'

The girl in the story – 'Jackie' I think I'll call her. Of course, Kylie down on the Reception Desk is my Jackie. It's time I stopped daydreaming and actually did something about her – something like asking her out. She's gorgeous. Mary, well she's not in the same bracket these days – sort of Stockport County to Man U thing.

Just how would *Arthur Randall* – Rod always liked to choose his characters' names early in the process – kill *Muriel*? Then how would he dispose of the body?

A few more notes were on the paper in front of him. *'Shoot? Strangle? Poison? If poison, what sort? Head and hands cut off to avoid identification. Feed bits to piranha fish. Keep rest in freezer. Take remains out in small boat and chuck overboard. How he kills her isn't important if no-one ever finds out – and they won't if there's no body to find. '**Dead Simple'**– good idea for title there? Missing wife? Explanation – she walked out on him. Marital differences public knowledge. Muriel has her own inherited money – enough for her to live on independently.'*

Nothing much too difficult to research if he looked in the right places. He'd start with Google – if they can't help, no-one can.

***

Normally Rod's 'homework' was done at his laptop. The following Saturday for a change he sat in front of a TV set to do his research. Cold and frosty outside, in a warm living room at home ready to watch the National Lottery programme seemed a reasonable place for many people to be. For Rodney though, it was a first. As was his purchase of a Lottery ticket down at the *Tesco's* near his office. He'd asked the woman behind the counter what had to do to select the numbers and how much it cost.

'I've got a virgin here' he heard her say to a colleague – 'he must the only man in the store who's never done it before.' He should be able to make a nice line or two in his new story out of what he'd overheard – maybe even a couple of paragraphs. Still, he wished she hadn't called out her comment as loudly as she did. People everywhere turning and looking at him was a bit embarrassing, to say the least.

Apart from seeing snatches of it when he happened to be in the room when it was on, the programme was all new to Rod. So he watched, remembering all the time he wasn't an ordinary viewer – he was a writer researching his next story.

Mary was an unwitting guinea-pig that evening – the victim-to-be hoping and praying that tonight would be her lucky night, the night she won the Big Prize. Her reactions to the televised draw were critical in the story, but his own feelings as he watched would be vital if he wanted to make his tale as realistic as possible.

The narrative he had already begun to plan upstairs over the last couple of days was being fleshed out and revised in his head as he sat there.

'Arthur watched Muriel with increasing disgust. She sat in her usual seat on the three-seater settee, the seat closest to the fire and the television set. She had kicked off her slippers and they lay where they had fallen, between her and the stone fireplace. Her legs were mottled by the heat from the gas fire. On the arm of the settee her right hand hovered over the Cadburys Roses box – the giant size, he noticed – and she dipped into it repeatedly. She didn't look to choose or select from the box; whatever her hand grabbed hold of went to her chocolate-ringed mouth. Already the box was nearly empty and he knew that she would have another one in reserve somewhere nearby. Silver foil wrappings were scattered around where she sat.

Muriel seemed unable or unwilling to watch silently, with the rustling of wrapping papers, the crunching and noisy enjoyment of her chocolates and her apparent inability to restrain from making comments about what was on the screen. Arthur knew from the rare, previously shared evenings in front of the television that what he was enduring was how his wife normally was when viewing – his presence there made no difference. She enjoyed watching television –he'd even heard her say with near disbelief that it was her hobby – and the noise she made while viewing annoyed her husband as much as her pleasure at what she watched baffled him. Mediocre entertainment at best, he thought, his wife obviously revelling in it.

He pictured the scene as it would be a few months ahead. He and Jackie – together – in their own little love-nest. Instead of that woman he'd grown to loathe, the fat – (no mincing words Arthur, you know it's true) – the fat, slovenly, lazy, woman she'd become after over twenty years together: instead his darling Jackie would be there with him. Just the two of them. Jackie – everything Muriel wasn't. Slim, beautiful, vivacious, amusing, intelligent and sexy.'

Were all of these qualities in his beloved really true? Rod didn't know. In fact he knew hardly anything about her. All the virtues that he attributed to Kylie were assumptions based on nothing more than a nice smile back from her in response to his regular 'Good Morning'. But his angel looked so ravishing, so pure, so stunning, so beautiful, that no-one who looked as she did could be less than perfect. So what if I am twenty-five or so years older than she is - a man can dream, can't he?

Seeing Mary looking like a beached whale on the settee made his need for Kylie more and more pressing. Next week – no Rod, that's not good enough, a vague 'next week' won't do – first thing on Monday morning he'd make his move on Kylie/Jackie. He'd had a good line in chat in the old days and a bloke doesn't lose a talent like he had back then. It must be like riding a bike – it's something you never forget. Just see her, charm her and arrange that all-important first date. Life's beginning to look better already. All except for that gross creature just a few feet away from him that he married when he didn't know any better. Thank God there were no kids to bother about.

Rod was increasingly baffled by what he saw on the screen and his wife's reactions to it all. The word 'Rollover' was mentioned constantly – meaning next to nothing to Rod but clearly a lot to the studio audience and to Mary who gave a little shriek each time the word came up.

'Now what you've all been waiting for – here and all you good people watching at home – This Week's Winning Numbers. Somebody somewhere is going to be a whole lot richer tonight. It might be you. Good Luck to you all. Here We Go.

When the smooth young man everybody in the studio audience so obviously adored uttered these words at what even Arthur could see was the highpoint of the show, Muriel for a moment or so stopped eating her chocolates.'

Torn between trying to see his wife's reaction and what was happening on the screen Rod did his best to take it all in. Mary had a number of tickets – ten every week he remembered her saying once, not that ten quid was anything to her after all her father left her – and had fashioned herself a little clip-board to have them all in her view as the winning balls began their journeys to end up in a tube. Rod assumed that the numbers in the tube he could see were the winning ones – something that was confirmed by these same numbers up on the screen and an excited voice calling them out. The whole process seemed to flash by yet go on forever. There they were – 1, 7, 13, 25, 26, 38.

'Shit.'

Mary's single word of frustration was passionate but suppressed. Unused to having her husband with her like this in the evening, she'd almost forgotten his distaste for anything he thought of as vulgarity. She tore the slips from the clip, scrunched them up and dropped them on the floor. Rod, knowing Mary's attention was on the events in the studio, looked at his own single ticket. His numbers matched those flashing away on the screen. It took a moment or two for Rod to control himself and to decide instantly that the win would stay a secret.

‘So, what happens now? If somebody wins a big prize how much will it be then?’ Mary turned and looked at him, surprised to hear his voice. It was the first time either had spoken since Rod had sat himself down at the opposite end of the settee earlier – something that happened so rarely she was still puzzled by it.

‘Well, tonight’s a Rollover so there’s extra money for a winner. There’s a show later on tonight when they tell you how many winners there are for the big prize and how much they’ve won. I usually watch it if it doesn’t clash with anything else.’

‘Arthur looked across at the long tank on its stand against the side-wall. There they were – his tropicals – his small collection of guppies, a pair of angel fish, the glinting neons in their own never-still world, and down at the bottom a catfish grubbing away. Harmless, gentle creatures.

But piranha fish like those he’d seen in that James Bond movie. Horrible brutes – like miniature sharks from what he knew of them. Still, he wouldn’t have to take ‘em for walks or anything – just buy as many as he wanted for a specific job then he’d get rid of them. Perhaps trade them back for some decent tropicals to add to his collection. All he’d need would be a new tank somewhere, probably in the garden shed – then they’d go. And so would the evidence with them. Perfect.

After he’d cut off her hands and feet they wouldn’t be much of a problem. Just lower the bits into the tank on a metal chain and then leave the rest to the piranhas. Probably starve the fish for a day or two before just to make them even more ravenous. Lift out the chain with just the bones of the hand left on it and voilá – the evidence has gone the way of all flesh. Well done, Arthur. Nice line that – ***‘way of all***

flesh'. *Might do for a title. Getting rid of the head – well, just see what you learn from watching the hands being eaten. Same principle though, just feed the fish when they look hungry. In fact, instead of all the bother with a boat to dispose of what's left, why not just cut her up and let the fish have all of her? It would just take a bit longer, that's all.*

Then after Muriel had gone he could do what he liked. Just allow the story that she'd left him to get around and be accepted – everyone who knows the two of them would probably express their surprise that she had gone and not Rodney – and let time do its work for him. Jackie's would be the shoulder to cry on, and what happened later would seem inevitable.

Remember Rod, money's no object any more – and it would be yours. No need to go cap in hand to that woman ever again. Tropicals by the dozen – whatever he wanted. There's plenty of room for more tanks round the place – that's if they decide to stay in this house. Jackie might well want something bigger and better than a three-bedroomed semi. A move to the seaside, go to live abroad, whatever. Anything his darling asked for she could have.

***

'Now I've seen it I'm just a touch curious to know how it all turns out, that's all. Let me know later on what happens – I might even start buying a ticket like you do. I'm popping out to the pub for a pint.'

Down at the *Green Man* the talk was all of that day's football. Malcolm Chambers came in for his usual drink just minutes before closing and joined in.

‘They could do with whoever won the Lottery tonight down at the City Ground. Just one winner and he’s won a fortune – nearly enough to buy half a striker at today’s prices.’

Rod finished his drink and went home. There was a message on the telephone table from Muriel that just had a pound sign and numbers on it – £14386293. He switched on his laptop, went to Google, and typed in his request. Among the options he found what he wanted *‘Piranha fish – all you need to know about them.’*

Just one more thing to do then turn in. He reached down the Yellow Pages and there they were – the people over in Miston he’d dealt with before.

‘TanksALot Exotics. We supply anything for the aquarist. The more challenging your need – the more we like it.’

Then just what he hoped to see.

‘Open Sundays 11 – 5.’

***

Muriel was grunting and snorting away in her own bed when Rod went to his. He lay there in the dark, smiling and happy. Today had been an extraordinary day. Tomorrow, well think of it as a workday. A working Sunday, Rod, with things to do – a phone call to sort out the details about his winning ticket and all his millions, then a few purchases to make. But Monday – Monday was really going to be a very special day. Yes, I’m looking forward to Monday.

SHOULD I KNOW YOU?

(Published in *Fiction on the Web*. June 2014).

Tuesday 23rd. 3.33 pm

'Right, you're all here then. I'll come straight to the point and it's bad news. At the end of the month this office is closing down and we'll all be unemployed. The firm's been taken over and everything is going online from a call centre up in the North East somewhere. No exceptions – everybody here is in the same boat: me included. Apparently it's going to be national – every branch office is getting the chop. The new people will give us what money we're entitled to – please don't ask me for details – I don't have them. There'll be a little bit extra on top as well, I'm told, so that will help. A man from Head Office will be coming down tomorrow or Thursday. He'll have individual letters for each of us with all the details. So there you have it. That's all I know at present. Under the circumstances I'll stick my neck out and say that anyone who wants time off for interviews and things will be given it. Sorry folks, that's it for now. Don't ask me questions as I don't have the answers. You now know as much as I do.'

'No, not now Fred. Ask the man when he comes tomorrow.'

***

5.58 pm.

Two cars had had a shunt and blocked Disraeli Street near the bridge just before rush hour. It didn't look serious – no ambulance or anything obvious – but it caused a tailback. Ian was stuck in it and couldn't turn round to go another way, so as he opened the front door he knew he was in trouble. Twenty minutes late. Good excuse or not he braced himself for a tirade.

‘Sorry, dear, there was an accident that blocked the road. Nothing I could do about it. Sorry.’ Instead of the ear-bashing he expected there was silence. The house was in darkness, and chilly with no central heating on. With an empty table in the dining room and no signs of food preparation in the kitchen, Ian became increasingly uneasy. Relief came when he saw the envelope on the mantelpiece in the living room. The single word Ian in handwriting he instantly recognised, and he gave an immediate sigh of relief. His world changed in the next few seconds.

I have left you. Peter Millbrook and I have today moved away from Sinfield. Where we are now doesn't make any difference to anyone else. Our marriage has finished. It should have ended a long time ago but I felt sorry for you and stayed when I should have gone. The only regret I have is that I'm telling you in this manner rather than face to face. If you haven't seen it coming, the signs were there under your nose and you should have. Peter and I have been in love for over 3 years now. If you want to contact me I still have my mobile. One good thing about this is we have no children to bother about. We should have had but when I checked with a doctor he said my side of it was fine. So, like almost everything that went wrong, it was down to you.

I suppose you will be bitter but let us try to be civil and civilised about it. You won't see me again – except maybe in court at the divorce I assume you will want. I won't be greedy and asking for a lot of money – just what I feel is mine. After that Peter has enough for both of us.

What you tell other people is up to you. For my part I won't tell anyone about the bloody awful marriage I've had to a boring, unexciting, feeble, pathetic apology for a man that you are. You're not

30 yet, but you've been middle-aged for years. You're a wimp, a loser. I shall never know why I didn't spot it before we ever married.

Convention says I should sign this 'with affection' or something, but I can't be that much of a hypocrite. What I feel for you is pity more than anything else.

Jane.

Ian felt as if he'd been hit in the stomach by Mike Tyson. As he always did at moments of stress he fingered the scar near his jaw, a reminder of infant school and a playground fall.

Lunchtime. The same day.

'I know that's your regular seat, Ian. You should grab it before it goes. Full for a Tuesday, aren't they? How are we then? Jane alright today?'

Ian mumbled something as he sat down then busied himself looking at the menu as he tried to cover his confusion. Small place, with just eight tables – but Ian would swear that he'd never seen this chap before. From his regular seat in the corner, exactly where he was sitting now, he could see everyone in the room – and this guy? No, never. Shabby, more than just a bit down at heel, dirty beige mac, needed a haircut, not shaved for days by the look of it. That grey stubble on his chin looks a right old mess. Grubby: the sort of chap who if you called him a dirty old man you wouldn't be far out. No, not here in the *Miramar* – he'd stick out like a sore thumb. And the clientele was a youngish lot while this old chap must have been well into his sixties.

The waitress came over and Ian gave her his order. The man nodded approvingly, 'Good choice. If you find something you like – why not stick with it? Beans on toast is your thing – so, as they say everywhere these days, 'Enjoy'.'

Ian knew full well he was a man of fixed habits, but finding that a complete stranger knowing apparently that he had the same meal two or three times in the week was a bit unnerving.

The man started eating, so for a while he didn't speak. Looking at him again, Ian became increasingly sure he didn't know him. Should I ask him who he is, how he knows me, or just leave it and expect never to see him again? Yeah, that's it. Do nothing and chalk it up as a weird happening.

Then the man spoke again. 'Jack Cunliffe. Do you see him about much these days? You remember Jack down at Fareham's? Must be getting on a bit now, old Jack. He had that back problem for years, of course. Still, no point in me telling you that, seeing you've worked at Fareham's for what – ten years now, isn't it? I know it was a January you started but I can't remember whether it was ninety-three or ninety-four.'

He'd finished his meal and topped up his teacup – no milk and no sugar, Ian noted approvingly – at least they had one thing in common. Then he stood up. 'Just before I go lad, a word of advice from someone who knows. Been there, and been round the block a few times. No matter how bad things get for you, try and fight back. I didn't and look at me. You still have time and the chance to get it all together again. Don't do what I did.' Just before he finally went he came out with a remark that puzzled Ian as much as anything else he had said. 'No woman is worth that much.'

The old man went to the pay desk, then walked out without another word. From the pavement he looked back through the door – Ian was still there at the table, just sorting out some money for his bill. Wistful, sad, regretful, concerned; it would be hard to put an exact word to the look on his face as he watched the younger man. Finally, shaking his head sadly he walked off, fingering the scar under the stubble as he did so.

EVERY PICTURE TELLS A STORY.

(Published in *Winamop.* March 2014).

'There's something up here that might be important, Guv. I'll fetch it down for you. You won't want it burying for ever under all that insulation, I reckon.'

The voice wakened me from my doze. A moment later I was handed a white cardboard shoebox, wrapped around with a navy ribbon. 'It was round the back of the cold-water tank – it looked as if it had been put there and forgotten. I'm off now. The loft job is finished. I'll be here same time in the morning to finish off the other bits and pieces.'

Sam *'No job too small'* Wilkins went out through the kitchen saying something to Win as he went, and left me holding a box and its contents I thought I'd lost for good.

I quickly undid the ribbon, saw the assortment of folded papers, photos and envelopes and things – all apparently in the same condition as they had been years before when I'd seen them last. No time for more then as Win came in with a tray of sandwiches. I know better than to pay less than full reverence to anything that comes from her kitchen so I closed the box.

'Win. You remember that box of her bits and pieces that my mother gave me just before she died? The one that went missing so I never really had a chance to go through and sort out? Well it's turned up in the loft. Mr. Wilkins found it just before he went.'

'You mean the box you lost, dear. Fine. Nice lady your mother. I always liked her.'

After we'd finished Win popped out for a chat with Sue – I could never properly remember her surname. When Win spoke of her it was always *Sue Next Door.* That was my opportunity for some peace and quiet for an hour or so.

Photos first, I thought. Right on top was a photograph in grainy old black and white on shiny card with curled up corners. It was the only one I ever had of my parents wedding. There they were – a short, stocky, severe-looking middle-aged man and the young, pretty woman who was inches taller than her husband. He had a flower in his buttonhole and she was holding a little bunch of something. The two were staring into the camera with the unease people often have in formal, posed photographs. It was clear the ceremony had been in a Registry Office and not in a church. I already knew it was a wartime wedding in the days of austerity.

I had just picked up the second picture in the pile and had begun to study it when I heard a key in the kitchen door. Win's voice called out – 'Next door's cousin from Newark has turned up. I've left them to it.' That was the end of the box for now.

Even so I'd seen enough on the second photograph to get the old memory cells going like mad. I was in it and it took me back donkey's years. I'm sixty-six, and there was I was, about eight years old so you can do the maths for yourself – that would date it about '50 or '51. Anyway, if I'm going to tell you the story of the photo I should go right back to the beginning.

We were living in Lincoln at the time. My father, mam and me. It was in the school summer holiday and the weather had been hot and dry for several days. I knew something special was happening as I heard my parents whispering together and then if they saw me listening they'd stop or talk about something else. Anyway, about teatime this particular afternoon mam told me that that I had to go to bed early that night as we were going off to the seaside next day and I needed all the sleep I could get. It was just to be mam and me. Father worked for the County Council and was very busy in his office – he couldn't spare the time to go away with us.

Before I went to bed mam looked out all my best clothes, checked them over and laid them out ready for the morning. Then she put whitening stuff all over my plimsolls and left them to dry overnight. I rummaged around for my bucket and spade and made sure they were where I wouldn't forget them in all the excitement when we were ready to go. In the morning I saw father giving mam some money – I think I saw some pound notes, crisp ones as if they'd just come straight from the bank – then he went to work. Minutes later we went to the 'bus stop on Kelling Road. Even though it was just a short ride to the station mam let me go upstairs and I stood at the front and held on to the metal bar at the window all the way. At the station mam joined a queue, bought the tickets and we went on the day excursion train to Sculthorpe.

We got there sometime in the late morning. I had a list of things in my head – things that mam had said we were going to do and I could have – and I was determined not to miss out on any of the promised delights. Ice creams, a ride on the donkeys, a play on the sands with mam helping me to build a sandcastle, lots of bottles of pop, and fish, chips, bread and butter and tea in a proper sit-down café (the tea would be for mam, of course – I was going to have something different – after all tea was an ordinary, everyday drink, wasn't it?) As far as mam was concerned all these delights had to wait. First she insisted on rubbing something on my face, and the same oily stuff on to my arms and legs before we left the station, then it was to be *'a nice cup of tea'* for her to start off the day. Me – well I had a big glass of dandelion and burdock with a straw. Then we made our way through all the crowds to the promenade and had our first look of the day at the sea.

***

It was later on, in the afternoon, very hot, and we were having a smashing time. We'd just been to see the Punch and Judy show and mam was tired and wanted a sit-down. She managed to find two empty seats, plonked herself down in one and put her bag on the other to save it for me. I remember wandering off to the big rail that overlooked the beach, but staying in sight as I'd been told to. Then I went back and found there was a man sitting in my seat. Mam spoke.

'This is Mr. Bennett, Richard. He's an old friend from back when I was at school.'

The man stood up and we shook hands formally like father had always told me to do. Mr. Bennett was a very tall man and as he spoke he smiled at me.

'So you're young Richard, eh? My name's Richard too. And how old are you then, young man?'

'I'm nearly seven and three quarters now. I'll be eight on November 10th. My birthday's on a Friday this year.'

He looked across at mam and repeated what I had said.

'Eight in November, eh? Is he a good boy then, Marge? Do you think he deserves an ice-cream then for being a good boy for his mother?' Mam nodded and Mr. Bennett reached into his pocket. He held out his left hand and passed me something. When I tried to take whatever he had it was an empty hand. Then he opened his right hand and there in the palm was a shiny shilling. 'Go to the kiosk there at the corner and buy the biggest cornet he can find for you.' He winked, stooped down towards me and his voice dropped to a whisper – 'And I don't want any change either.' I ran over to the little cabin and had to join a queue to be served.

When I got back mam and Mr. Bennett were talking quietly. I was busy with my cornet and trying not to spill any on my new shirt and wasn't listening, but I seem to remember hearing some of what they were saying. I heard things like 'how was I to know?' 'had to move away,' 'no address,' 'Lincoln,' 'Mr. Grant.' And there were other words that I didn't understand. They both looked very serious about something.

Mr. Bennett stood up. 'Young Richard Grant. Why don't you, me and your mother have a picture taken? Come on, Marge – it'll give me a souvenir of today.' He put his hand in the air and called out to the man with the camera and black shoulder bag who was patrolling nearby.

He went over to the man and they spoke. 'He wants us walking. He says it's more natural and makes for a better snap.' The three of us; mam, Mr. Bennett and me in the middle holding hands with both of them did our best not to look too silly and self-conscious with our smiles as we walked towards the photo man.

'I've told him we're here just for the day and he's going to rush them especially for us. I'll see him right for his extra trouble, of course.'

Taking me by the hand and grabbing the beach ball I'd bought that morning, my new friend took me down the steps onto the beach, and we happily played football till mam called us from up above. Mr. Bennett found the photo man, handed mam her copy of the picture, went to the kiosk again and bought me a stick of rock. White inside, pink on the outside with Sculthorpe printed inside it in a curve. It was very sticky and crunchy on the teeth I remember. Mam put it away in her bag to take back home with us. ‘I’d had enough for now’ she said. ’If you have any more you’ll be sick on the train going home.’

Then it was time to go and Mr. Bennett insisted on walking to the station with us and he bought a special ticket that let him go through on to the platform and the trains with us. As we said goodbye he pretended to put his right hand up to my face and he found a shiny half-crown in my ear. He did make me laugh. Mam didn’t look very amused though, I think she must have been tired out by then. From the platform he waved and I waved back until he was out of sight.

On the way back mam made a big fuss and showed me how I looked in the mirror she had in her handbag. My face had gone all red and mam said my nose would look like a ripe tomato in the morning. She said that father wouldn’t recognise me looking like that but I knew that he would so we laughed at what she’d said.

I wanted to talk about Mr. Bennett – for instance why was she *‘Marge’* to him but always *‘Marjorie’* to my father – but mam said she needed a little nap so she turned away to go to sleep. I must have dozed off, but remember that when I woke up mam was looking out of the window. I could see her reflection in the window and she looked sad. We’d had such a lovely day too. It must have been because our little holiday had nearly come to an end. Then she saw me looking at her and smiled at me.

Then mam said things that I’ve never forgotten. I was only a child back then, but even if I don’t get all the words right I remember what she was trying to say. ‘We owe everything to your father. He’s been as kind to you and me as any man ever could be. He doesn’t show his feelings very much, and he doesn’t make a fuss of you like some fathers do with their children, but he loves you very much. That's something you must always remember.'

***

All this reviving of long, half-buried memories started me thinking. Next morning – remember I'm retired so I'm my own boss and can do what I want when I want, except when Win's around of course – so I had a quiet time on my own. Yes, she who must be obeyed was round with *Sue Next Door*. So I lifted down the box for another look at its contents.

I looked again at the wedding picture then turned it over and looked at the back. There was an address on it, the sort of thing you do with a rubber stamp and an inkpad. It gave the name of a photographer in Leeds. There was also a handwritten date in black ink. I scrabbled into the box and found what I wanted. A yellowing single page document that most of us have, or will have sometime or other – a *Marriage Licence*. *William George Grant* to *Marjorie Thelma Burnett.* The date matched the date on the back of the photograph. I didn't need to find the other document. Like everyone else, I knew my own birthday. So when my parents married I was already fourteen months old.

So the old dog had jumped the gun had he? That he had didn't bother me in the least, but no doubt back then it must have caused serious problems for the two of them. Society was different in the nineteen-forties. Stigmas were attached to events that no-one seems to bother about any more these days. No doubt it would explain the Registry Office wedding and might even explain why the family home I remember was in Lincoln and not in Leeds.

***

It was the following Sunday morning. Our son Jimmy, Margot and young Rick were with us for lunch. I was taking a quick glance into the shoebox when Rick came into the room. He's twelve, bright as a button and can wrap me round his little finger. I know it, he knows it and he knows that I know it.

'Caught you, Grandad. So this is where you hide all your secrets. How much will you give me not to tell Nan? It must be worth fifty pee? Honestly though, if they're anything to do with the family I'd like to see them. I watched a programme the other night about family trees and genealogy and it was fascinating.'

I tried to close the box with 'Another time, Rick' but he was too quick for me. He picked up the picture from Sculthorpe. 'Well then. There's a lady and I think that's you so that will be your mother, my Great Grandmother. Is that right, Grandad? Very pretty, wasn't she? And the man must be your father – anybody can see that. You're so alike. You, dad and me – we're all tall. I'm nearly six feet already.'

Rick picked up the old photo of my father and my mother on their wedding day. 'And the old man in the photos with Great Grandmother when she was young? He doesn't look like anyone else in the family. Who's he then?'

'He was elderly gentleman who was very good to my mother and me many, many years ago. He died when I was about your age. I didn't get to know him as well as I should have and now it's too late. He was a very kind, very generous man and I wish now I'd got to know him better. And you're quite right, Rick, he wasn't any blood relative – more a sort of in-law. You know, honorary family, related to us by marriage.

Had Rick been a few years older I might have told him the full truth. That's what I tell myself anyway. I should have: after all Rick was mature enough then to take it all in and understand the implications. But I didn't. Should have, but didn't. Trying to protect my long-dead mother's reputation? That's what I told myself anyway. But I shouldn't have lied to him like that.

PROBLEMS, PROBLEMS.

(Published in *Scribble.* Summer 2012).

I'm a man with a couple of problems. I've a deadline to meet this weekend, so one of them needs to be sorted very quickly – the other is slightly less pressing. So let me introduce myself and tell you what they are. After all, who knows, you might be able to help me.

I suppose I should really say *'Hello, hello, hello.'* In my day-job I'm Detective Sergeant Pardoe, member of the CID in one of England's largest cities – Rick to my friends, Mister Pardoe to the low life I meet every day – but readers of *Mature,* the UK's best selling magazine for women of the fifty plus generation, would know me as *Prunella Joyce.*

No, I'm not a cross-dresser, transvestite or any of the variations on the theme that you may have heard of, I'm simply a normal bloke who has found a niche for himself in the very limited world of the short-story market by pretending to be a woman. They're sworn to secrecy down at *Mature*, while on the job they know I write a bit – after all, they are detectives – but I don't want them to know that Rick Pardoe, hard-nosed, hard-drinking cop, writes gentle, nostalgic tales set in a time-warp village somewhere in the Cotswolds where the biggest crime imaginable is to drive at 32 in a 30 mph zone. You can imagine how much stick I'd get from that lot after a pint or three. After all, they call me *'The Jeffrey Archer of Tollis Street nick'* – and they mean that as a compliment too.

In the Job I've done well. My track record is streets ahead of any of my contemporaries round here. I can catch thieves the good old-fashioned way, something that pleases many of the old school who are still left, and yet I know how to play the game with the new breed of 'managers' – well enough that is to be thought of as one of their own and looked on with extreme favour. I'm well on with my studying for the Inspector's Exam and I'm confident – but not too cocky – about the result when I do sit it. With early promotion likely sooner rather than later my career is on the up and up. There is that bit of a problem with my partner Debbie, but I'll come to that later.

This business with me writing as a woman. Like all hopeful, part-time authors I write when I have some spare time, something which there isn't a lot of in my job where regular, predictable fixed hours and shifts are from a world the humble copper can only dream of. I had a couple of stories accepted writing as myself, then I wrote one, then another, based on middle-class people living the sort of lives I imagined comfortably off, slightly snobbish people would lead in the cocooned society of an olde-worlde village in one of the prettiest parts of England.

After I'd put something down on paper and had a considered look at what I'd written I began to see the possibilities of sequels and even a series. Already a couple of ideas for further episodes were buzzing round in the old brain-box and I knew I was on to something. I even had hopes of a TV adaptation – it's the sort of thing the Beeb could do well if they put their hearts into it.

So, what to do with what I'd written? From my dealings with different editors I knew which ones wouldn't want it. So that ruled out three of my regularly targeted magazine contacts: Matt Murdoch, Peter Hodgson and the nice people at *Cameo* who are a writer's dream by usually replying to submissions within days. Then my moment of inspiration. Mentally I gave myself a sex-change and looked at listings of what was aimed at the female readership, an area I hadn't seriously looked at before. To cut a long story short – no pun intended – I approached *Mature*, and they snapped up my two stories and the idea of a series. And they pay well too. It's a monthly bookstand issue thing and so far I've had twelve of my stories published in it.

This leads me to Problem Number 1, the one I need to sort out quickly. I have two of my characters – Nigel and Hermione Babbington – the names seem right for the sort of people they are – and they're mulling over what to do about the Annual Fete down in the village. They're very keen to get their friend, and moderately successful author, Miles Trelawney, to open the proceedings. He doesn't sell massively but his reviews are excellent in the posh Sunday's. They want to put one over on their arch-rivals, the Fortescue's, who have this particular pal they're pushing for the role. He's slightly better known from the telly, but he's from Sky, so that's a black mark against him in the eyes of several of the Committee. By Saturday evening I have to decide and wrap up writing and email the finished article. Even as I mention it to you now, I think I really have already made up my mind what I'm going to decide on where the story's going. So, let's just forget what I've already said and I'll tell you about my other problem.

This is a biggie. As I said, I'm keen on promotion and it can't be far off, but with it will come a transfer to another division, possibly even another force. Inevitably that will mean putting my house on the market and moving on. And Debbie, my partner, is in the way. She's blocking my hopes for advancement by simply being there in the house with me.

She's being stubborn about the whole business. I've tried talking to her, reasoning with her, but she just looks at me and says nothing. Absolutely nothing. Not a single word. In fact it's quite a while since she said anything at all.

When we first met and she moved in with me, nearly six years ago now that'll be, she would talk the hind legs off a donkey. But not anymore. And there's a hygiene problem too – the sort they used to say in the advert something like '*and would your best friend tell you about it?*' To put it delicately – Debbie has B.O. I've told her about it as discreetly as I can but there's no doubt about it – she doesn't smell as sweetly as she should these days.

She's losing weight as well. Every time I look at her she seems thinner that she was. Of course, she never will put weight back on till she starts eating properly.

I cook specially for her too – eggs, bacon, sausages, fried bread, a '*Full English*' – the lot. All the stuff she used to love. And every morning I take it down to the cellar for her – nicely laid out on a tray. Pot of tea and toast too if she wants them. But she doesn't eat a morsel. Whatever time I get home, down I go and what do I find? The same tray, exactly where I left it – untouched – and Debs still in the same place, just giving me that same look with her head twisted over to one side. I'll swear she never moves an inch. The last time I saw her move was the day we had the big row, and that must nearly three weeks ago by now. Every day she just sits there looking reproachful as if it was all my fault.

After all who started it anyway? But how can I put my house on the market with a sulky, silent woman who smells a bit down in the cellar. A woman who won't even speak to me to discuss it. Now, you see the problem I have to sort out. So, I ask you – what would you do if you were me?

WHY CAN'T THEY LEAVE THINGS ALONE?

(Published in *Fiction on the Web*. April 2014).

Would you buy a used car from a flashy, smooth-talking salesman called Ambrose? I wouldn't. But my wife fell for his patter and now she's my ex and living with him in Basingstoke. And good riddance too. So Charlie Medwin, that's me, on my own for a few weeks now, had a few adjustments to make in the way things went. By now I've pretty well sorted out my new routine. Take shopping for instance. Vera used to do what she called her 'big shop' down at *Tesco's* on Friday evenings. Not me. Now there's a lot less needed, and anyway, I've got my own way of doing things. She paid at the checkout for everything she took from the store. I don't. I pay for what's in the trolley and everything else is a nice little earner for me.

Chissingford where I live is big enough to have the lot – *Morrisons, Sainsbury's, Tesco's, Asda,* a *Co-op* of course, even a *Waitrose* – the one they call *'the toff's supermarket'*. No continental stores yet, but it's only time, isn't it? So I've got a bit of a choice when I shop. Of course, I don't look for *2 for 1* offers and that sort of thing. No way. I just look where it's the easiest to steal from. The supermarkets are getting better on their security these days – in fact, there's one of the big boys I don't go near anymore – that is unless I'm being an honest member of Joe Public at the time and queuing up at the check-out like the ordinary punters. Which one? No way, José. That's for you to find out. After all, it's taken me a long time to get all this know-how and I don't give info like that away for free. Now if you offered to pay me for what I know – well, that's another matter.

With all the new rules ciggies have become very difficult these days. So I don't try. I leave them alone on their locked shelves and concentrate on the bottled stuff – they all have masses of wines and spirits on their shelves. Then CD's are usually a piece of cake to lift, and if you pick the chart stuff they're dead easy to shift. And every penny is profit. No overheads, nothing like that to worry about.

The main things to look out for are the 'hidden' cameras – now that really is a joke. With the exception of one store – no names, no pack drill – where they aren't at all bad, whoever decides where to place them seems to have no idea, and if you know what to look for they're no problem. As for store detectives, most of 'em haven't a clue; just see 'em a couple of times and you remember their faces. In my experience, unless the bosses are around they've usually switched off and are working on autopilot.

If I were honest – get it? – I really believe I could save the typical supermarket chain serious money by advising them on what to do: sort of poacher turned gamekeeper thing. My proposal would be for them to agree to pay me a Consultancy Fee of, well, let's say 20% of what I would save them in a typical year. They'd be quids in and it would certainly suit me. As a pro I'd know what to look for. I've seen other people doing what I do in their stores and you can pick 'em out easy. The difference is I don't think the people I spot would spot me doing the same thing. Rank amateurs, most of 'em. They haven't a clue. Perhaps I should approach one of our local store managers with my idea. Prepare a proper case – the sort of thing they call a Business Plan, on paper with figures and everything – and see his reaction. Just a thought. After all, they tell us that the best hackers in the business are working now for the internet security companies or at the Pentagon. It makes sense, doesn't it?

As I said, my methods are my own and I won't divulge them to anyone else. Let me just say that I'm good at what I do and, if you want proof, get someone to look in the records of the local constabulary. Not once have I been pulled in for questioning, never mind being charged. My sheet is completely clean. It's a matter of professional pride to me even though I know you straight folks probably don't approve. Eight years doing what I do and the only blemish on my record is a parking fine – and they don't count, do they? My old dad was a regular in the army and always said that Long Service medals and Good Conduct badges just recognised a set number of years of undetected crime. He was probably right.

***

On Wednesday morning it all happened. At about eleven fifteen, I was down at one of the stores on the Cherry Lane Estate – I won't say which one but you could easy check if you wanted to – and had just gone through checkout number 4. They were very busy and the girl on the till apologised about the time we'd been kept waiting. The woman in front had been a bit silly with a lot of money-off coupons and things, and wanted to change items, and one of the store girls was sent off to do it for her and it all took time.

Well, there I was, checked out and everything, just heading for the exit when these two guys in suits and a uniformed man pounced on me. That's my lot, I thought. I've been spotted. I had a proper receipt in my pocket for the stuff in the trolley, but I had somehow overlooked paying for the two 1 litre bottles of Glenfiddich, and some Rioja that were in the big, deep pockets of my coat. Decision time. Should I brazen it out or go quietly?

I didn't have much choice. The older man, bald, horn-rimmed glasses, in a natty suit and with a large badge in his lapel, held out his hand, started to shake mine vigorously and somewhere just out of my vision a camera started flashing.

'Congratulations, sir. You may not have realised it, but you are the ten thousandth customer this store has had since we opened. As such all your purchases today are free, with our compliments, and we would like you to be our guest for a little ceremony. It won't take more than a few minutes and you will be given a momento of the occasion.'

Everything I'd just bought was free! If only I'd known. There'd be a lot more than eight pounds forty three penceworth in my bag (a reusable one, naturally, as I like to do my bit for the environment). Mind you, if I'd taken longer choosing I would have been further back in the queue and not the magic number – so there you are. Sod's Law in action.

People gathered round at a little table near the main entrance. Mr. Mallinder, that was his name, droned on a bit, and some smarmy looking guy in his best suit fawned all over him. I found out later that Mallinder was from Head Office and the creep was the store manager. Afterwards they showed me all the pictures they took and creepy had managed to get near his idol in every one.

People were clapping, pictures were being taken, some girl with *'Press'* on her blouse asked me a few silly questions. I was very good and showed great self-control. I answered all her questions as best I could, but didn't do what the badge said, even though she was a big girl – if you know what I mean. So apart from the made up selection of groceries and a special something – that was it. The special? An extra large bottle of Glenfiddich, wouldn't you guess it? And I'm teetotal at that.

End of story except that I was heavily featured in the press as a result of my little surprise. Just the locals, of course, but in the *Chissingford Recorder*, the *County Gazette* and both of the free advertising rags. Pictures and a big plug for the store. So, that was my fifteen minutes of fame that apparently we're all going to get some time in our lifetimes. Not that I was over-pleased. Living the sort of life I do the last thing I want is publicity. I certainly don't want my face plastered all over the place and being seen by people I don't want to see it. Something I'd do my best to avoid in future – no more exposure again if I can help it.

***

It didn't work out quite like that. I was in the papers again not long afterwards. This time the nationals got in on the act with a whiff of a story from somebody local and enjoyed themselves at my expense. In the *Mirror* they decided that *'On the house? Not this time, Charlie'* just about summed it up. The *Sun* typically used just one word – *'Stupido'*. I'm fairly thick skinned but their comment about me writing a book *'Shoplifting for Dummies'* hurt a bit.

Stupid on my part, perhaps? I don't think so really. Only with 20/20 hindsight. No way did I think they'd challenge me back at 'my' supermarket. Any member of staff who'd been working that day would almost certainly have seen me at my little 'do', and my photograph was prominent in a display at the main door and they all knew I was on the VIP list. And having seen the old geezer they'd stuck a uniform on and called security – well, it was a piece of cake. Back at the presentation either the two bottles of scotch, or the vino I hadn't paid for, I don't know which, had clinked in my pocket when I was about two feet away from him, but he didn't seem to notice, or more likely, he didn't have his hearing aid switched on.

He'd gone and they had a woman down there now, didn't they? Just my luck she was on duty when I went shopping – someone I'd never seen before, fresh to the area and ex CID. New on the job and still dead keen to get some brownie points. Probably paid on commission for every one she pulled in. If she'd been on duty the day I won my big prize I'd have spotted her for certain. It turned out she had only started with them that Monday, just days after me being the toast of the store with everybody. Talk about luck.

When it came out that I had been taking stuff on a regular basis, the bosses made a few changes. Among other things they downgraded Mr. 'Smarmy pants' Poulson and posted him up north somewhere. So it wasn't all bad, was it?

By the way, I did have a word with the new manager. I made my offer of some advice on shoplifting on a Consultancy basis. He didn't actually say *'No'* but somehow I don't think he was keen even though I offered to drop my fee down to 15% for him.

***

Actually, when it got to court I thought I'd had a bit of a raw deal from the magistrate. She was a hatchet faced woman who seemed not to like anyone, and even though I put on my suit and a tie, it didn't do me much good. When she heard I'd been doing it for years, she gave me a twelve month prison sentence, suspended for two years.

That was worse than a fine actually. If I'd been given a straight fine, I'd have paid it at a fiver a week, and the slate would be clean and nothing carried over to be held against me in future. That's the way I saw it anyway. But this probation deal meant that if I did the business and was caught, anytime in the next two years, I'd go inside. What Mrs. Thomas Fitzwallace, MBE, JP, B&Q and bar, or something fancy like that, hadn't realised was what a sentence like that was really going to cost me. The duty solicitor the police had given me said I'd had a good deal but I didn't see it like that. There's one law for them and one for people like me. No wonder I left the court fuming.

My personal cost of living was going to go up sharply for as long as I am on probation by paying the same prices at the check-out as ordinary punters do, and it's criminal how expensive stuff is these days. And it's going up all the time too as I soon found out. Because of this woman I now have to pay for everything I shop for every week Perhaps the old cow did realise it and was just being sadistic. She certainly looked the type. Then she hadn't made any sort of allowance for my loss of income from the stuff I sell on, none whatsoever. I've got to fill it from somewhere.

So it looks as if I'll have to find a new line of work. Pretty soon too. Back to the drawing board and sort out a Plan B. I'm the wrong shape for climbing through windows to half-inch a bit of jewellery, and hitting old ladies on their heads for their pension money isn't my style, so that's not on either. But I'm certainly not looking for a proper job just yet. I'll leave that for when I'm really, really desperate.

TWO PIECES OF FLASH FICTION.

(Published in *Winamop.* February 2015).

What is called 'Flash fiction' has no hard and fast definition. I personally think of it as a story of no more than 200 or so words.

***

'Eve?

Yes, Adam?

Yesterday after that snake creature spoke to you I saw you talking to a woman down at the far end of the garden. Was that your mother?'

***

'Noah, you keep telling me that a voice has told you what to do about the animals when the rain stops. That you're going to let them out to start breeding. But are you sure that you've picked the right couples for the job? For instance, I'm a bit concerned about those horses with a single long horn sticking out of their heads – have you ever had any second thoughts about your choice of Tristram and Gerald?'

And finally…. The following is not a short story.

I wrote the piece for *Scribble,* the short story print magazine that publishes quarterly with a consistently good selection of tales, hoping that it might help an aspiring writer. There was some feed-back. It did point someone in the right direction. .

Please note. The title was chosen by *Scribble* – not by me.

THAT'S THE WAY TO DO IT.

An article published in Scribble. June 2014.

Why do I think I am qualified to help aspiring writers? Because over the last seven years or so, I have been there / done that / got the T shirt as well as the scars; and by doing things wrong I have found out how to do them right. My credentials are, to date, 26 short stories accepted for publishing by various magazines – including 4 here in Scribble. The first twenty of these I have put out as a collection on Amazon / Kindle. In addition, also on Amazon / Kindle is a full-length crime story, and in preparation is a collection of more published stories and a number of novellas that are too long to send to short story magazine editors. I accept that using Amazon is self-publishing, but, regarding the unsubmitted novellas, I feel I am as severe a critic on myself as any editor. And perhaps even more important as part of the learning curve – to have 26 stories accepted there have been many, many rejections, each one of which teaches a lesson.

So, with my cards on the table here goes.

Obviously, it's no good me going on about where to look for an outlet for your masterpieces until they are written and ready. So let's start there. Let's take it that you have a couple of stories completed and, in your view, as the proud author, they're ready to go into the big, wide world.

The first thing I would do would be to put them away for a while; do something else and forget them. Then, when you have left a few weeks between completing a story and the last time you read it – then read it again. You may well be surprised. Probably you will see little things that you have missed before. Possibly something major, like a discrepancy when Edith becomes Ethel from Page 3 onwards, for instance. Or a complete non-sequitur that is nonsense when you look at it with fresh eyes. Then you will probably see ways that parts can be improved – create another paragraph break, or change the sequence of events to make a bigger impact. Or just written differently and better. And the alternative ending that was at the back of your mind when you were writing – perhaps it would be right after all. Also, unless you're infallible, it's almost inevitable that the odd typing error will be there. Blame the keyboard – I always do. Years ago, when Bill Gates was a mere boy, I was covering musical events for a newspaper for several years. Using an Olympia portable typewriter, the number of times I cursed that the machine could not spell 'Mozart' – and back then it was two sheets of paper with interleaved carbon paper to correct it. At least these days, typos can soon be put right. Incidentally, all my suggestions are made on the assumption that you use a computer.

I usually read out loud what I have written as if it's a short story on radio. That way I get the feel of the story's rhythm for any rewriting that may be needed – particularly for speech. You may also find an adjective is overused.

So, let's assume you have the finished article. Does it look good? Is it tidy and presentable? Try to see it from the viewpoint of the person you will send it to. Have you set your indents for the first line of paragraphs? Personally I set my machine up for an indent of 1 cm. Incidentally, for a long time I made a mistake by indenting the opening para of a story. Only later did I realise that it, and the first paragraphs of any chapter, should not be indented. Line spacing – normally double for me. The grisly world of Headers and Footers is not too bad once you've been there a few times, but if you're sending a story for submission electronically – don't bother (unless it's asked for). If you are sending by snail mail to Scribble, for instance, or another magazine; then number pages at the bottom centre from Page 2 onwards, and title the pages (top centre) using a small font (8 or 9). I prefer to italicise page numbers and titles as I think they look more professional that way. The normal font I use for the body of the story would be Times New Roman, Size 12, with the main title bigger – try 14 and see what you think. Finally, I set for justified text – the one that fills the lines evenly and that looks a lot less straggly on the page.

Now you're ready to go. My first look for an outlet would be by using *Duotrope* – https://duotrope.com/search.aspx. It was free but they now charge, but the cost is, in my view, worth it. That is until you have built up your own personal list of likely magazines contacts – then you can cancel *Duotrope*. Think of it as a search engine – a sort of *GoogleWrite.* Using its powers, you can nominate the genre and length of what you want, get it to throw out a selection for you, and then save the list for future use. My setting for the search is pretty wide-open – I have opted for 'Any genre', 'Short story'. Submission - 'Any type' (allowing for submitting by post or electronically, the latter always easier for the writer, and increasingly the norm these days); Subject 'Any.' In addition I have opted for 'UK' in Country – otherwise the list the system throws out is much too big and unwieldy.

Then with the list on screen, you read through what is said about the relevant titles, follow the links to the Web Sites and make your choice. Don't rush it. The key things to look for are stipulated word length and type of story the editor is looking for. The editor of a Fantasy Mag won't appreciate your story about domestic discord in Amersham – you are wasting your own time as well as his. Carefully read the submission guidelines and take care to do all that he/she wants – even though this may mean revising your own carefully done formatting. Sending a specially good piece off as an attachment when they clearly want something in the body of an email is not the way to make friends and influence people. Most editors want previously unpublished material – sometimes there is a box to tick – but anyway I usually make a point of telling them that it is. Also, personally I normally send a little covering message – don't try to be too formal. Editors almost invariably will try to get you to buy a copy of their magazine *'to familiarise yourself with what we're looking for.'* Unless it looks overall like something you may want to send to regularly, why bother? If you have your own style and method, I would stick with it and not try to change for a particular outlet. I accept that that this is contentious and the choice is yours.

Chasers – or as I have seen them called –'queries.' The sort of small magazines we're considering here are almost all run on a shoestring, often by volunteers. So, the last thing they want is to be chased too early for a response. Normally, unless the website says otherwise, I would allow 3 months before sending a polite email asking at what stage things are. Some replies will have already come through by that time lapse, but I find no-one resents being asked nicely by then.

Let us assume that by now you have two, three or more stories out on offer. Before the numbers get too unwieldy I should make sure you have a decent system set up to keep track of your material. If you have emails coming and going it is so easy to get mixed. Start sooner rather than later.

Rejections. They're a fact of life and we must learn to accept them. If it helps, it isn't unusual for Editor A to write 'Sorry, but' only for Editor B to snap your hand off and want to buy the screen rights. Sometimes an editor will offer a reason why he doesn't want your story – more usually not. But for all the rejections you have – when an acceptance does come along, it makes it all worthwhile.

Enjoy your writing – and the very best of luck.

H.D.